Hi all... Thanks x

More emails from a toxic school

Volume 3 – The Two Fingered Kitkat

Hi all,
Last week's Teacher Of The Week was to have been Mrs Davinson.
She refused to accept the two-fingered KitKat because she's a
coeliac and doesn't believe in chocolate, apparently. Because of her
disrespectful behaviour, she's been given a letter of Management
Advice.
Thanks x

Hi all,
Tomorrow's guest speaker has had to cancel. Not to worry, though,
this means that you can spend two extra hours in Departments
planning for Tuesday. Just kidding, we're doing ice breakers.
Thanks x

Hi all,
To help the environment and keep the car park looking more like
Fortnum and Mason and less like Home Bargains, we will be taking a
leaf out of Mr Khan's book and charging anyone in a non ULEZ
Compliant car £12.50 to access the Academy car park from
tomorrow.
Thanks x

Hi parents,
You have exactly 2 days to get your kids ready for school. Fake nails
must be removed, coloured hair back to normal, acceptable shoes
(not trainers), and just because the woman in Ann Summers said it
was a school uniform, doesn't make it an Academy uniform.
Thanks x

Hi all,
Some of you have emailed me to complain that, on reading the new Behaviour Policy, you have found the name of another school. Well, I can tell you we did that on purpose. There are 5 other schools mentioned in there. Find them all and win an indoor duty point.
Thanks x

Hi all,
Just to put your minds at rest, none of The Academy buildings have been made with crumble-risk concrete. Our buildings are really not that good. Most of them are made of chicken wire and old porridge. Don't worry, though, none of them has fallen down yet.
Thanks x

Hi all,
Before this morning's CPD sessions, log on to the new VLE. For security reasons, all passwords must be changed. They must contain at least 8 letters, a number and a special character. All passwords must be shared with your HODs and then emailed to your link SLT.
Thanks x

Hi all,
To get you ready to return to The Academy, we're going to help you practise getting up early. We've been allowed access to the Government's COVID Siren thing and will be messaging you tomorrow and on Sunday every 5 minutes, starting at 4:45am, until 8:30am.
Thanks x

Hi all,
Thanks to those who sent in planning for the first term. Sadly, you didn't check this morning's email with the new format. The new layout must be landscape, narrow margins, comic sans 12, in dark grey (not black) and with The Academy logo in colour on every page.
Thanks x

Hi all,
Don't forget that Monday's CPD day starts at 6:30am. We've so many ice breakers to get through that, if we don't start straight away, we won't be able to finish for 8pm.
Thanks x

Hi all new staff,
It is customary for one of you to ask a stupid question right at the end of our First Day Back CPD. If none of you volunteers before Friday lunchtime, one of you will be chosen at random.
Thanks x

Hi all,
Due to non-payment of subscriptions to our reprographics provider, we no longer have photocopiers at The Academy. You really should be doing everything electronically anyway. And think of the time you'll save, not queuing at the copier on Monday morning.
Thanks x

Hi all,

Thanks so much for all of your hard work today. Such a shame we didn't have time for any planning. Don't worry though, The Academy buildings open at 6am, which gives you a couple of hours before Briefing to get it all done.

Thanks x

Hi all,

The students are back in The Academy from today. Can tutors please do uniform checks and contact parents immediately if there are any issues. Refer any angry parents and disgruntled children to Pastoral Heads and not SLT. We have much more important things to do.

Thanks x

Hi all,

Today's Deep Dive of KS3 and KS4 English has been postponed until next term. I know some of you were here until after 10 o'clock last night. I hope you didn't spend too much time preparing. I'd be furious if that happened to me. LOL.

Thanks x

Hi all,

In order to keep the smokers and vapers out of the toilets during lessons, our new caretaker, Mr Johnson, will be releasing a dozen or so wasps in there at the end of each break time. If it works, we'll try it out in the pupils' toilets, too.

Thanks x

Hi all,

The surveyors have been into the kitchen and given it a clean bill of health. What we thought could have been RAAC turned out to be old mashed potato, which has apparently been there since the Great Kitchen Explosion of 2018.

Thanks x

Hi all,

After yesterday's incident when Boy Jayden escaped from the Remove Room by attaching himself to the underside of Mrs Johnson's Hot Chocolate Friday Trolley, we've decided that distributing hot reward beverages will now be the job of at least 5 members of SLT.

Thanks x

Hi all,

Don't forget that it is Academy Policy that 90% of our students need to be achieving above average if you are to pass this year's Appraisal.

Thanks x

Hi all,

Some of you have queried the timing of today's full staff online 2 hour Time Management CPD. It obviously isn't today at 1pm. We're not monsters. That was a clerical error. It's today at 3pm.

Thanks x

Hi all,
After one of our new Year 7 pupils almost choked to death on a pen lid, we have decided to ban all pens in The Academy. Pupils will be allowed to use pencils in their lessons and 9Z will continue to make shapes in the air with their fingers.
Thanks x

Hi all,
Our New Staff CPD sessions are going well. Tonight's meeting is on using The Academy's North Korean Sims knock off, tomorrow is Assessment and Examinations and, on Wednesday, Mr Johnson will show you how to avoid the CCTV when attempting to steal KitKats from the canteen.
Thanks x

Hi all,
For Health and Safety reasons, pupils will no longer wear their ties during practical technology lessons. To avoid any accidents, all ties must be put in pockets. Sadly, the pupils will all get a negative Classcharts point for not wearing a tie. Them's the rules.
Thanks x

Hi all,
Thanks to all of you who sat patiently and politely in yesterday's CPD when Mr Johnson told us how to make excellent soups, roasts, frittatas and omelettes. We thought we had booked him to talk to you all about Coping with Asperger's, not Cooking with asparagus.
Thanks x

Hi all,
We have decided that our new feedback code for pupils' redrafted work, "A Reasonable Second Effort" should be scrapped immediately. Please do not write ARSE on any more of their books.
Thanks x

Hi all,
Our SLT in charge of Displays and Corridors has spent 2 days checking displays. Using a spirit level, he has discovered that every department is breaking the "horizontal staples at 180 degrees" and "vertical staples at 90 degrees" rule. You must sort this out before tomorrow.
Thanks x

Hi all,
With the next set of Year 11 GCSE mock exams starting on Monday, we've decided not to use the Main Hall as this causes too much disruption. We will use the top floor of the main building instead. All maths and geography classes will move to the gym for one week.
Thanks x

Hi all,
We have finally discovered why the Year 7 students keep getting lost around The Academy. Apparently, the Academy Map in the front of their homework diaries is not a map of The Academy at all but a schematic of the first level of the PS5 game, Baldur's Gate 3.
Thanks x

Hi all,

The remaining Exams Analysis Meetings will be held in the Main Hall tomorrow after school at 4pm. The Principal is losing his voice and is so sick of shouting at Heads of Subject, that he has decided to get you all together and have just one big rant instead.

Thanks x

Hi all,

Can you please make sure that you send all of your up to date email passwords to HR as soon as possible. Some of them didn't work when we tried to read your emails.

Thanks x

Hi all,

Apologies for all of you who were waiting for the Employee of The Week Award to be announced today. We didn't bother this week as Miss Johnson was away on a NPQSL course and it was her turn to win. She'll get her KitKat on Monday.

Thanks x

Hi all,

The 1st set of GCSE Mocks seems to have gone well. They must be marked for Monday's moderation CPD. Please use exam board mark schemes and grade boundaries. Remember even though they've only done half the course, we expect all pupils to be hitting their targets.

Thanks x

Hi all,
You may have seen the news reports about the violence caused by, and the imminent eradication of, XL Bullies. We feel we should clarify that this refers to the dangerous dogs and not Boy Jayden and his cousin, Keanu.
Thanks x

Hi all,
There's a new SLT post on The Academy website. The job title is: Senior Leader: Assessments and Grades. If you see yourself as The Academy's next SLAG, see Carole for details. Our last SLAG, stepped down after realising she'd bitten off more than she could chew.
Thanks x

Hi all,
You may have seen other Academy Trusts in the news counting the pleats in girls' skirts during uniform checks. We will not be doing this. Instead of wasting time on this, plan some better lessons. Most of your lessons are really awful.
Thanks x

Hi all,
The third week back sounds like a good time to have a crackdown on shoes. Girls should be wearing black Clarks T-bar sandals and boys should be wearing Clarks Wayfinders. Please check that the compasses in the Wayfinders heels are calibrated to magnetic north.
Thanks x

Hi all,
Tonight's New Staff CPD "Dealing calmly with all behaviour situations" will start a little later than planned. Mr Johnson has had to go for a lie down in a dark room after threatening to punch Boy Jayden's lights out when he called him a "fat old paedo".
Thanks x

Hi all,
Just a reminder that this term's first Mocksted will be tomorrow. Like the real thing, we won't be letting you know when or who we are coming to observe, but it won't be anyone who achieved a positive GCSE residual this summer.
Thanks x

Hi all,
Please congratulate Daniel Johnson in Year 8, who has just qualified for the World Youth U16 Chess Olympiad. Even though his selection has nothing to do with us and we don't even have a chess club, our CEO will be on the local TV news with Daniel this evening.
Thanks x

Hi all,
Remember that, in The Academy, we never say that a child is failing an exam or a course, we always use the phrase "Working Towards". Also, tomorrow afternoon we will be publishing a list of all the staff who are "Working towards" UPS.
Thanks x

Hi all,
Please congratulate Miss Johnson on her promotion to subject leader. She will be our new Head of Economics. You've no idea how difficult it has been to find someone with the skills and qualities needed to be an outstanding HOE.
Thanks x

Hi all,
Tomorrow is Year 7 Open Evening. It is Directed Time and, just like last year, we expect "all singing all dancing" demonstrations, displays, examples of work and performances from PE and Music. Let's hope that some people actually turn up this year.
Thanks x

Hi all,
We know what the strange smell on the 1st floor is. At first we thought it was the disabled staff toilet, where Mr Johnson is making a batch of his home brew but it's coming from the kitchen. They've started cooking sprouts to have them ready for Christmas lunch.
Thanks x

Hi all,
Next week we meet our new PGCE students. Three of them look about 12 years old and probably won't last until half term. There's also a tall, muscular and handsome PE teacher, Mr Johnson, who we already have earmarked for an SLT post next September.
Thanks x

Hi parents,
Apologies for, yet another, error in this week's Academy Newsletter. On Monday, pupils will be receiving their annual flu jabs, not anal flu jabs. Although this could be arranged.
Thanks x

Hi all,
Thanks so much for all your suggestions on how we can make the staff room more welcoming. We have taken your ideas on board and decided to use them all. Now, it's so nice, only SLT will be permitted to go in there from Monday.
Thanks x

Hi all,
Today's Mocksted went well. We now have a clear vision of what we need to do in order to improve in The Academy to get that elusive "Good" Ofsted judgement. Sadly, it involves getting rid of most of the staff and almost all of the kids.
Thanks x

Hi all,
Unfortunately we've had to close down 9Z's lucrative Friday home bake stall. There have been a few complaints in the past about the proceeds not reaching the ferret rescue but, yesterday was the final straw when the sultanas in their scones appeared to have legs.
Thanks x

Hi all,
You may have seen our advert in the TES for an Antisocial Behaviour Coordinator. We are pleased to say that we have had a lot of applications, mainly from 9Z's parents, but unfortunately, almost all of them seem to have misunderstood what we are looking for.
Thanks x

Hi all,
After Mrs Johnson's nervous breakdown, we need someone to run the Chess Club. It's on Wednesday lunchtimes. You don't even need to know the rules. It's mostly kids from 9Z throwing chess pieces at each other. The first to draw blood shouts "Checkmate" and wins.
Thanks x

Hi all,
Tonight's CPD is Behaviour And Leading Learning Strategies. Mr Johnson will be coming from The Trust to talk BALLS to us for two and a half hours.
Thanks x

Hi all,
Don't forget that tomorrow is our Year 7 Settling In Evening. Parents will need to know how their children are getting on, what GCSE and A Level results they're likely to get, which University they'll be going to, and the career they most likely to excel at.
Thanks x

Hi all,
To pay for the rebuild of the SLT Lounge (formerly the Library)
we've acquired some sponsorship. From today, each of your
PowerPoints must have the Day-Glo Dragon Energy Drink logo in the
top left corner and it will now be the only drink available in the
canteen.
Thanks x

Hi all,
You may have seen our good reputation being besmirched in the local
media and on the socials by angry parents spreading rumours. Can I
remind you to tell your classes that we have never won the Worst
School in Britain Award. We only came second. Twice.
Thanks x

Hi all,
We have put together a list of our children who could use extra help
in core lessons. These Pupils Requiring Intensive Coaching for
Knowledge will be taken out of MFL lessons by their coaches. There
is a list of all the PRICKS on the staffroom wall.
Thanks x

Hi all,
Our website has been hacked again. The letters NPQH after the
Principal's name stand for "National Professional Qualification for
Headship", and not "Never Present, Quite Horrible".
Thanks x

Hi all,

We have decided to make duty points more accurate and will be using the What Three Words app to tell you where you need to go on duty. Sadly, due to a typing error, the History Department will be on break duty on the big roundabout on the ring road just outside Copenhagen.

Thanks x

Hi all,

Thanks to Tina and Janice for taking the time out of their holidays to try to improve 9Z's literacy skills. I hope the Reading Festival lived up to their expectations and that they managed to find a lot of new books for The Academy library.

Thanks x

Hi all,

We start back at The Academy in exactly one week. This week would be a good time to start practising not eating all day, not going to the toilet between the hours of 7am and 4pm and yet still managing to drink 5 huge Sports Direct mugs of lukewarm instant coffee.

Thanks x

Hi all,

We still haven't managed to find a new SENDCO for September, so we have asked Carole in the Main Office to do it. How difficult can it be? Surely, it's just a matter of ordering different coloured exercise books.

Thanks x

Hi all,

Remember that certain fragrances are only to be worn by SLT within The Academy. SLT women over 30 must wear "Burberry Brit" and under 30s "Colleen". Men must wear either "Joop Homme" or "Drakkar Noir". This will help us to identify staff before we see them.

Thanks x

Hi all,

Due to an autocorrect error, rather than receiving a class set of iPads, as promised, you'll all be receiving a class set of ink pads. At least you'll be able to collect their fingerprints on the first day back.

Thanks x

Hi all,

Many of you have emailed asking for class lists. We'll get them to you as soon as we can, but our priority at the moment is getting the timetables finished. That and finding 29 new teachers to fill all our vacancies before the end of next week.

Thanks x

Hi all,

Now the GCSE results are in, I can start to create the new duty rota. If you achieved a positive residual, your duty point will be inside, close to your classroom. The Geography department will be on duty outside the Coop in the next village, when it's raining.

Thanks x

Hi all,

The Summer Holidays Computing Club seem to have mixed feelings about the retro games consoles we bought for them. Some of them preferred playing on the Commodore 64 but the autistic kids were all on the Spectrum.

Thanks x

Hi all,

Just to let you know that Chantelle's little sister will be joining us next term. Despite being excluded from the PRU, we have decided that she deserves a second chance. She has some anger issues, her own personal TA and, ironically, she's called Hakuna Matata.

Thanks x

Hi all,

Today is Results Day and we are celebrating our best results ever. Our number of students receiving five 4-9 grades is almost in double figures. If we knew what Progress 8 meant, we'd probably be celebrating that, too. Well done to SLT for all their hard work.

Thanks x

Hi all,

Tomorrow is Results Day. Only SLT are allowed on the premises between the hours of 9am and 2 pm. If you don't normally wear a shiny, blue suit and brown shoes or a black, mini skirt suit with 5 inch heels to work, you will be prevented from entering by security.

Thanks x

Hi all,

We have a vacancy for a car park supervisor. Duties include making sure staff park in the right place, emptying the foreign coins and buttons out of the ticket machine and issuing fines to anyone parked over, on, or near the lines. This is an SLT post. M9.

Thanks x

Hi all,

Due to an infestation of rats or cockroaches, or possibly both, The Academy kitchens will be closed for the foreseeable. For the first week back, please bring your own lunches and enough for the children in your tutor groups, too.

Thanks x

Hi all,

Can we please remember that, even though the first day back is a CPD Day, we still expect certain standards of attire and appearance. Last term, it looked like we were hosting auditions for The Walking Dead.

Thanks x

Hi all,

In the past, we have been accused of, and criticised for, labelling some of our less academic students. However, since 9Z found that old Dymo machine in the English stock cupboard, they've spent most of their time labelling themselves.

Thanks x

Hi all,

As nobody has volunteered to be 9Z's form tutor next term, we have decided to have a lottery. This replaces last year's Battle Royale which "the unions" say is, apparently, not the way to treat professionals.

Thanks x

Hi all,

I've just received this memo from Mr Johnson, our Head of PE: "Now that football isn't coming home, we are going back to netball for all girls' PE lessons. Football is for boys."

Thanks x

Hi all,

As Monday is a bank holiday, our work shy site team are taking the day off and refusing to open the school (unless we pay them). This gives you two choices: Teach online lessons or, weather permitting, teach your classes on the sports field or in the car park.

Thanks x

Hi all,

It was nice to see so many of our pupils, especially the girls, all excited getting on the coach for today's Hamilton trip. I didn't realise that so many of the children in our drama group were fans of Scottish League One football. Up the Accies!

Thanks x

Hi all,

We're ditching We All Now Know as our plenary task header as, apparently, the acronym is a bit rude. (Why did no one mention it?) Luckily, Miss Johnson, has come up with a new idea: This Is Today's Subtopic. I hope you'll all become fans of Miss Johnson's TITS.

Thanks x

Hi Year 11,

If you haven't already received an invite to Results Day, you won't be allowed in. We only want the good looking, photogenic ones in The Academy, just in case the local press turns up. Aesthetically challenged students will get their results by text.

Thanks x

Hi all,

Because the Catch up, Revision And Practical Lessons you put on have been so successful this holiday, we're going to carry on teaching CRAP Lessons at The Academy every day next term.

Thanks x

Hi all,

There's been another typo in the new Academy Magazine. The sentence in question should read: "Our new MFL teacher, Mr Johnson, has a first class degree in Greek" and not "Our new MFL teacher, Mr Johnson, is a first class Geek". We can only apologise.

Thanks x

Hi all,

Remember that only SLT and visitors are permitted to use the main Academy entrance. UPS and TLR use the side entrance, MPS around the back and Support Plans through the Art room window with the broken catch.

Thanks x

Hi all,

Even though we don't have a 6th Form, we do have a pupil expecting A Level results tomorrow. Dylan Johnson, in Year 8, has completed A Levels in Maths, Statistics and Pure Maths. Obviously, his dad coached him through it but we're taking all the credit.

Thanks x

Hi all,

Some of you have been complaining on Social Media that the pupils are not turning up for your Catch Up and Revision Lessons. From tomorrow, it is your responsibility to get them to attend. Start by ringing parents, then have a long hard look at your lesson plans.

Thanks x

Hi all,

From next term we are reintroducing the Staff Planner. An A4 page for every lesson must be completed and will be checked by your line manager, who will use your plans when doing book scrutinies. They cost £25, which will be taken from August's pay.

Thanks x

Hi all,

You have been emailed the new revised Staff Handbook. It's just 700 pages. You must read it and email your line manager to confirm this by 3pm tomorrow. I hope you can all still open Amstrad Wordstar files?

Thanks x

Hi parents,

Please be aware that string bikinis are not suitable attire for swimming lessons at The Academy.

...and Cheese String bikinis are even less suitable.

Thanks x

Hi all,

To save some money, we have decided not to use professional window cleaners around The Academy next term. Individual teachers are responsible for their interior windows and Mr Johnson from PE will be relaunching Bungee Jumping Club to clean exterior windows.

Thanks x

Hi parents,

Please stop telling us how to run The Academy in your badly thought out TikTok posts. Just because you occasionally went to school doesn't mean you could run one.

Thanks x

Hi all,

From September, our newest Assistant Head of Something Or Other, Miss Johnson, will be presenting a series of CPD sessions on Teaching and Assessment. Our CEO is already getting excited at the prospect of T and A with Miss Johnson.

Thanks x

Hi all,

Can the more ambitious among you please stop asking us to fund your NPQH courses? We already have one Needy, Pathetic, Questionable Headteacher, we don't need any more.

Thanks x

Hi all,

From September, we've decided on specific colours of exercise books for each subject. If you have already bought books, you will either have to return them and order new ones, or swap with another department. Also, the Finance Office is closed for two weeks.

Thanks x

Hi parents,

Here's a quick reminder of our uniform policy: Academy blazer, white shirt, Academy tie, black trousers or skirt, black shoes (not trainers). It's really not that difficult. Pupils not conforming will be sent home. Unless they're in Year 11 or called Chantelle.

Thanks x

Hi all,

Next Wednesday, The Academy will closed to all staff and students. We have hired a photographer and some blonde models in designer outfits, to smile like loons and jump in the air pretending they got good exam results. It'll look great on the website.

Thanks x

Hi all,

Mr Johnson is really excited about his new promotion to Head of our new "Public Relations Unit". Please don't ruin his holiday by telling him what PRU really means.

Thanks x

Hi all,

Even though the GCSE results aren't due for a couple of weeks, The Calendar says that your Departmental GCSE Exams Analysis is due in by 4pm today. Please email all reports to your line-manager who won't read it but will send you a receipt sometime in September.

Thanks x

Hi all,

When you return to The Academy you'll notice the staff room is now the Maths Department. It's a good size, will easily fit fifteen classes and the fact there are no walls means we can observe all the teachers at the same time. What could possibly go wrong?

Thanks x

Hi all,

In September we'll be trialling a new idea: Training Initiative for Teaching Staff Under Performing. I imagine most of your careers will go TITSUP after the GCSE results.

Thanks x

Hi all,

New Staff Induction Day went well today. We couldn't give them their timetables, do the Child Protection stuff, allocate classrooms, or distribute their ID badges or passwords, but they did a lot of the ice breakers they'll be doing again on the 4th of September.

Thanks x

Hi all,

Just a reminder that you won't be paid this month as you're not, technically, working. I'd pop into your bank and ask for an overdraft extension if I were you. We're an Academy, not a charity.

Thanks x

Hi all,

Due to the fact that we have not paid our utilities bills for quite some time, there will be no electricity or clean water in The Academy for the foreseeable future. If you're planning on coming in during the break, bring plenty of fresh water and a cardigan.

Thanks x

Hi all,

We are reintroducing "Pen Licences" for all students in September. A Provisional Pen Licence costs £43 and is valid for 12 months. Pen Tests can be taken at the end of each term at a cost of £62. Pupils can rack up points for messy writing and speeding.

Thanks x

Hi all,

There is an error in this week's Staff Newsletter. It says "From September, registration will be at 8:30 every day." This obviously doesn't include Saturdays and Sundays, when Catch Up Classes registration will be at 8:45.

Thanks x

Hi all,

Just a reminder that the 1st set of Year 11 mocks starts on the 5th of September. All exam papers need to be prepared, checked by line managers and photocopied before the end of next week. It must be a full GCSE exam even though they haven't finished the course.

Thanks x

Hi all,

We have made a slight miscalculation and forgotten to add Year 11 to next term's timetables. We just assumed that they wouldn't need one because they left in June. Anyway, new timetables will be out in a week or so and you're all losing two frees. Oops.

Thanks x

Hi all,

Contracts state that all teachers must change the displays in their classrooms and in corridors every two weeks. As most of you haven't been in since the 21st of July, you'll need to be in this week getting it done. Let's hope you're not already on Support Plans.

Thanks x

Hi all,

Summer School is going well. So far we have had five of our new Year 7s turning up at 8am to take part in a packed schedule to learn The Willows Way. We have also had almost 100 more arriving just in time for lunch and leaving just before one o'clock.

Thanks x

Hi all,

From September we'll be adopting a new mantra in our vain attempt to reach an Outstanding Ofsted grade. This time it's Culture, Respect, Awareness, Pride. The Academy will be so full of CRAP in September, you won't recognise the place.

Thanks x

Hi all,

To save money we're restructuring again. Heads of Department will lose their jobs. They'll be replaced by two SLT positions, Head of Core and Head of Non Core. Current 2nds in department will become Subject Organisers and do the old HoD job for half the money.

Thanks x

Hi all,

Please remember that, from September, every piece of work will be marked using our new formula: Assess, Review, Share, Evaluate Success. We will be regularly checking books and displays to check that pupils are aware of the real impact of ARSES on their futures.

Thanks x

Hi all,

To save money and the environment, we've replaced the staff room and library photocopiers with monks. They'll copy out worksheets for you and even do the first letters in really big, fancy writing. They need 6 months' notice for a class set, 8 if it's in colour.

Thanks x

Hi all,

If any departments have not yet applied to have a PGCE student next term, you must contact me this week. A good student teacher can bring so much to your department and save The Academy a fortune in cover.

Thanks x

Hi all,

We have found a new stationery supplier. It's a company owned by Chantelle's "Uncle" Dave. They operate from the same warehouse as Educational Supplies Ltd, but after 11pm, round the back and it's cash only. If we save enough, we can keep that TA until Christmas.

Thanks x

Hi all,

We notice that some of you were in The Academy last week decorating your classrooms. While this is commendable, and some of you have gone to a lot of expense, you haven't used Academy Trust colours. Some of you have even used last year's colours. Change it. Now.

Thanks x

Hi all,

Now that the unions have voted to accept your, not fully funded, pay rise we need to start looking at redundancies. Obviously, we'll start with Humanities, MFL and Art. If you can think of any others, don't hesitate to inbox me.

Thanks x

Hi all,

Good news: we have discovered where the gas leak was coming from and can continue with today's Summer School. However, due to a minor explosion we have decided to relocate the Food Tech room to the second floor. That's where most of the appliances landed.

Thanks x

Hi all,

From September can we please go back to using our Verbal Feedback Given stamps? If Mlle La Rose of the MFL Department could stop writing "Oral Given", that would be great, too.

Thanks x

Hi all,

Our Teaching and Learning Leader has come up with a new award. The Writing And Numeracy Knowledge award will go to the KS4 student who shows the most improvement. We hope getting a WANK from Miss Johnson will particularly motivate underachieving boys.

Thanks x

Hi all,

Depending on this year's exam results, we may be going back to a three year GCSE. If they're worse than expected, we're going to start 5 year GCSE courses, if they're OK, we'll stick with four years. There may be timetable changes. Again.

Thanks x

Hi all,

Next week is New Staff Induction Week. All Heads of Subject will be expected to attend, even if you don't have a new member of staff. Remember, you are not allowed to mention: Non negotiables, TLRs, CPD, the Time Budget, Break Duties, Salaries, or Chantelle.

Thanks x

Hi all,

After much discussion, we have decided to allow students to continue to vape in the first floor toilets. The smell of strawberry marshmallow mist is a million times better than the usual smell emanating from there.

Thanks x

Hi all,
Tomorrow we will be looking through this year's Prom photos and deciding which of our Year 11 pupils are photogenic enough to be photographed on Results Day. Pupils who don't make the cut will be asked to stay away. They'll be notified by their Head of Year.
Thanks x

Hi all,
As a reward for behaving and achieving so well and knowing that they really love drill music, we have a treat for the Year 11s. We've booked the Coldstream Guards Brass Band to play on results day.
Thanks x

Hi all,
We have had complaints from some of you that the new Willows Handbook has just been stolen from another school and just had the front cover changed. This, of course, was a test to check whether you really have read it. Congratulations.
Thanks x

Hi all,
Please congratulate Miss Owen who has been promoted by our CEO, Mr Johnson, to Assistant Principal. We've no idea who she is, what experience she has or where she's come from, and she looks like she's in her late teens. She's in charge of Policy and Appraisal.
Thanks x

Hi all,

Please be aware that all The Academy's buildings will be closed next week due to the exterminators coming in to solve the cockroach problem. All catch up lessons will be taught on the playing field, the basketball courts, or in the deliveries yard.

Thanks x

Hi all,

Due to a shortage of teaching staff, from September, tutor groups will contain 50 to 60 pupils. They will also not have a tutor but a prefect, a TA, or one of the invigilators left over from the summer exams. What could possibly go wrong?

Thanks x

Hi all,

Due to an unexpected lottery win, we have a vacancy for a Head of Year 7 for September. If you are a crazy and fearless lunatic, with a sense of humour and no sense of smell, you'd be ideal. Most of your time will be spent handing out tissues and dry underwear.

Thanks x

Hi all,

Thanks to all who came in for catch up lessons today. It all seems to have gone extremely well. Hopefully, some pupils might turn up tomorrow. If they don't we won't be able to pay you again.

Thanks x

Hi all,
Apologies for cutting short the Keynote Speech by Jayden's Uncle Gary during last night's Careers Evening. When we booked him, he told Carole he was going to talk about his criminal practice and she just assumed he was a lawyer.
Thanks x

Hi all,
Tomorrow's Year 10 GCSE Catch Up Sessions start at 9am. Staff need to be in at 8 to prepare, make breakfast for the PP kids and watch a short, pre-recorded staff briefing in the main hall at 8:30.
Thanks x

Hi all,
Due to a miscalculation, you have actually only completed 1264 of your contracted 1265 hours this year. Therefore we expect everyone in on Monday morning at 8am for an hour long briefing. Anyone not turning up will have their contract terminated immediately. Thanks x

Hi all,
We forgot to mention that there'll be a "deep clean" of all classrooms during the summer break. All your personal items will be clumsily thrown into an unlabelled box and left in a damp shipping container, which rats most probably fornicate in, before September.
Thanks x

Hi all,
We forgot to tell parents that we have changed the uniform and that blazers are no longer compulsory. Never mind, we can tell them in September. I'm sure that blazers aren't that expensive.
Thanks x

Hi all,
I'm sure you'll join me in congratulating Miss Johnson as she has now qualified as a Certified Leader Using New Guidelines in Education. She is extremely proud and would love to show you all her CLUNGE at every opportunity she gets.
Thanks x

Hi all,
If you're leaving The Academy this week, you can download a pre-signed leaving card from the VLE. There are 3 choices: 1) Flowers, 2) Humorous and risqué, 3) Offensive and containing the word "cockwomble" If you're printing it, please don't use colour. Or card. Thanks x

Hi all,
Today you're with your tutor groups. You'll use this time to explain the new behaviour and uniform policies. If you are a Year 9 or 10 tutor, you will go through the holiday catch up timetable with them. Year 7 and 8 tutors go through the 500 page homework packs.
Thanks x

Hi all,
There is the opportunity to say goodbye to the teachers who are leaving The Academy this week, at a get together on Thursday at the end of school. I won't be there. I looked at the list and I've never met any of them. It's directed time for you lot, though.
Thanks x

Hi all,
Please don't send any children to REMOVE on Friday afternoon. Apparently, 9Z have booked it for their End Of Term Bash. They're bringing home brew, snacks and are even decorating the booths.
Thanks x

Hi all,
I'm sure you'll all agree that the new, purpose built library building is quite amazing. In fact, we like it so much that it is going to be the new SLT Lounge. The library will move to the English Department stock cupboard, after the official opening by the CEO.
Thanks x

Hi all,
While we understand that parents are reluctant to buy new school shoes in July, we're having a crackdown on footwear tomorrow. If you can't see your face in them, they're not school shoes. Tutors will contact parents to explain why their child is in isolation.
Thanks x

Hi all,

On Friday we're having a barbecue. When I say "we", I mean the Senior Leadership Team (but not Assistant Vice Assistant Principals' Assistants, obviously). We'd be grateful if you could leave the premises the same time as the kids, before the catering trucks arrive.

Thanks x

Hi all,

Bad news I'm afraid. The "celebrity" we booked to give out prizes at the Awards Evening tomorrow has had to cancel due to getting a better offer. Therefore, Mr Johnson will do it, doing his Frank Spencer. If anyone has an overcoat and a beret, please let us know.

Thanks x

Hi all,

Behaviour update. Just a reminder that the "eye roll" is only effective when staff are not wearing their Academy-issue mirror lens sunglasses. You know the three step policy:

1) Take them off.
2) Roll eyes.
3) Point sunglasses at pupil in a threatening manner.

Thanks x

Hi all,

Great news! From September, The Academy will be taking part in Learning Action Zone Year for Assessment Research in Secondary Education. All of our teachers, who sign up, will be able to put LAZYARSE on their CV and all official correspondence.

Thanks x

Hi all,

Apparently visitors to The Academy are getting lost as we don't appear on anyone's Sat Nav. Please tell anyone visiting The Academy that if they use the What Three Words app, they'll find us by typing, "Abandon All Hope".

Thanks x

Hi all,

Before you start spending your national pay rises, here's a reminder that you're not employed as teachers, but Learning Facilitators. As an Academy we've opted out of agreed national pay levels and can pay you what we like. Read your contracts. Enjoy the weekend.

Thanks x

Hi all,

Monday's Mocksted has been postponed. We have reconsidered and decided that the beginning of the last week of term is a terrible time to have it. Therefore, we have moved it to Thursday.

Thanks x

Hi all,
Just a reminder that you must empty the staff room of all belongings by the end of school so the builders can start work on our Sensory Safe Space. This is primarily for our pupils with ASD, ALS, and cognitive disabilities. And Tina when she comes in hungover. Thanks x

Hi all,
Just a reminder that, at The Academy, we teach right up until the final bell on the last day of term. There'll be no fun lessons, movies, or wordsearches. If it's not in your Curriculum Plan, it's not happening. Unless you get 9Z. Do whatever you like with them. Thanks x

Hi all,
There has been another spelling error in this week's Newsletter. It should have read: "Our new Head of Food Technology, Mr Johnson, was previously a Master Baker". Apologies to him and his family. Thanks x

Hi all,
After successfully reintroducing the Teacher of the Week we have decided to reward support staff, too. So, each term we will be surprising someone with our new Teaching Assistant Recognition Trophy. Who will be this term's lucky TART? Thanks x

Hi all,

From March we have another new initiative: Trustwide Involvement in New Directives in Education Research. Each of you will be signed up and have a link to your TINDER profile on The Academy website.

Thanks x

Hi all,

We have discovered who is sending the "explicit" photos to HR. Carole was apoplectic. Janice said she thinks it might be an ex-boyfriend. Apparently, Mr Johnson cut himself quite badly last weekend and sent the photos as proof. Turns out it's a septic finger.

Thanks x

Hi all,

Tonight's CPD is a test of your creativity. Please bring with you an empty yoghurt pot, 15 different coloured pipe cleaners, a sheet of A4 sticky labels, a stapler, three styrofoam cups, a metre of string, and 3 glue sticks. If we start at 4 we'll finish by 8:30.

Thanks x

Hi all,

From September we are removing the comfy chairs from the staff room and replacing them with the creaky, collapsible ones from the exam room. Hopefully, this will stop you socialising during breaks and we can continue with our Divide and Conquer policy.

Thanks x

Hi all,

There is an error in the new Academy Prospectus. The sentence "Here at The Academy we have a no hair policy" should read "Here at The Academy we have no hair policy", meaning we are tolerant to all hairstyles, not that all our students should be bald.

Thanks x

Hi all,

Thanks to the generosity of one of our Academy sponsors, we now have brand new white carpets in the Art rooms, the boys' changing rooms and the Food Tech suite. This means that nobody will be allowed in those areas for the foreseeable future.

Thanks x

Hi all,

Some schools in our area have lost thousands of pounds worth of equipment after a spate of recent burglaries. In other news, Boy Jayden's Uncle Dave has donated 80 "refurbished" PCs to The Academy.

Thanks x

Hi all,

Don't forget, Monday is Meet and Greet Year 7 Tutors Evening. From 3:30 until 9pm, new Year 7 tutors will talk to the families of their new pupils, answering questions and making them feel at ease about The Willows. Let's hope someone actually turns up this year.

Thanks x

Hi all,
Year 7s loved the visit from the local zoo, especially the keepers' presentations, and the fact they got to stroke the exotic birds they brought with them. It's a shame Tina was on strike. She was only saying on Thursday she'd love to get her hands on a cockatoo.
Thanks x

Hi all,
Don't forget that we are keeping every child's exercise book in every subject for the next 18 years, just in case Ofsted wants to see them. Please make sure all your books are marked up to date and put in packing crates in the old drama rooms by the 14th of July.
Thanks x

Hi all,
Starting today, we are reinstating the Teacher of the Week Award. The prize will be a 2 finger KitKat. It will be chosen solely by me, purely on merit and most probably given to Mr Johnson, the new PE teacher in the very tight shorts.
Thanks x

Hi all,
We've been looking at the criteria for Prefects and have realised that everyone in the current Year 10 and Year 9 cohort has too many negative behaviour points. Therefore, we will be choosing our prefects and Head Boy and Head Girl from the new Year 7 intake.
Thanks x

Hi all,

After today's strike, we realised that we can open The Academy and still teach quality lessons to all classes with only half the staff. Therefore, we will be re-restructuring again before September.

Thanks x

Hi all,

Great news. We have been awarded Teacher Enrichment Specialist Training In Cultivating Leadership in English Schools status. We can now put the TESTICLES logo on our letterhead with pride.

Thanks x

Hi all,

Remember that New Staff Induction Week is the 3rd week of the summer break. We don't do it during term time as we don't want them to meet the kids before they sign their contracts. Heads of Subject must attend for at least three of those days, unless they're SLT. Thanks x

Hi all,

Thanks so much for your input during Monday's Schemes of Work CPD. Who'd have thought it would go on until 9:30pm? Just a reminder that if your schemes are portrait, you must change them to landscape and if they are landscape, you must change them to portrait.

Thanks x

Hi all,
Over the summer break, we will be replacing all of our IT equipment in The Academy. If you have an Academy laptop or tablet, you must return it "as new" and with its original packaging. If it is not "as new", you will be charged the full retail price for it.
Thanks x

Hi all,
Some of our ECTs claim they didn't know that, as a part of their contracts, they have to teach two weeks of Catch Up School during the summer holiday. It is on the VLE.
Thanks x

Hi all,
Don't forget that this week's focus is uniform. Any pupils breaking The Academy's Uniform Standards will be isolated for the day and parents informed that their child will not be allowed in lessons until they are dressed correctly. Wednesday is non uniform day.
Thanks x

Hi all,
We thought Just Stop Oil protestors had broken into the sports hall and put orange dye into the swimming pool yesterday. It turns out it was Tina. She went for a before school swim and accidentally washed off all of this week's layers of foundation and fake tan.
Thanks x

Hi all,
It's great to see everyone in The Academy winding down for the summer. Just three weeks left. Or, to put it another way, 4 twilight CPD sessions, 2 end of term concerts, 3 parents' evenings, 5 school show performances, a prom, 6 fire drills and 2 Mocksteds.
Thanks x

Hi Heads of Subject,
Can you please check reports carefully for spelling and grammar mistakes before they go out to parents? As far as we are aware, The Academy does not have departments called: Scince, Gography, or Inglish. Maths doesn't have an apostrophe, either.
Thanks x

Hi all,
Yesterday's Mocksted went well, despite the Year 6 Transition Day, Sports Day, the Sex Ed bus, the local primaries' athletics tournament and the Year 9 Mock GCSE exams. We will be deep diving Maths, History, Art, MFL and Science this morning, before break. Thanks x

Hi all,
Year 6 Transition Day was a huge success. Special thanks to Mrs Johnson who managed to keep September's 7Z contained for most of the day with only one incident. On the plus side, it was her first ever trip in a helicopter. Shame it was the Air Ambulance.
Thanks x

Hi all,
Tomorrow is staff photo day. This is for your ID Badges for September. Even if you're leaving you need to have it done, so security know who to turn away. Please dress smartly and if you're going to smile, please remember your teeth, Janice.
Thanks x

Hi all,
Don't forget that, due to a mix up on the calendar, the Year 7 Parents' Evening and the Nudists' Association Gymnastics Championships will both take place in the Main Hall from 3:30pm until 6pm. The school counsellor will be available from 6pm until 8pm.
Thanks x

Hi all,
Despite the warm weather we need to have a serious talk about skirt lengths. Quite frankly, it's getting quite obscene. Members of SLT will be coming into lessons tomorrow to speak to the worst offenders. It's a good job the kids don't dress like that.
Thanks x

Hi all,
We have had a good look at the end of year reports and we don't like the format. We have paid a graphic design consultancy to redraft them and will share this new format tomorrow. This gives you a 24 hour turnaround for you to redo them all for Wednesday.
Thanks x

Hi all,

Please congratulate Mr Johnson, who from September, will be taking on the role of Coordinator of Upskilling in New Technologies. He is keen to get started and we have already made the sign for his office door.

Thanks x

Hi all,

Don't give out any negative behaviour points to 9Z for the rest of term. There are so many, it's started to crash our servers. Just look the other way. Remember our behaviour policy: Step 10 is a negative point. You're forgetting the "eye roll" and "tuts" first.

Thanks x

Hi all,

We have decided that the best way for our pupils to show progress in all their subjects is to give them GCSE papers to complete every term from Year 7 through to Year 11. Anyone with a target of 9 will be expected to be achieving a 5 by Christmas of Year 7.

Thanks x

Hi all,

There was total chaos on this weekend's Duke of Edinburgh Expedition when the Year 10s found themselves at the campsite where one of the CEO's secret families lives. He was a little embarrassed to say the least. Anyone who mentions this will be fired or excluded. Thanks x

Hi all,
We've made an absolute killing selling Leavers' Hoodies to the Year 11s, so we have decided to sell Starters' Hoodies to all years. They cost £35 and will fund either a TA or a coffee machine in each SLT's Assistant's office. It'll help us learn kids names, too.
Thanks x

Hi all,
The Uniform Lost Property Mountain is unsafe and getting out of control. It is the only man-made structure clearly available from space. Students and staff have until Tuesday to claim their possessions and then the Eco Club kids are going to torch it.
Thanks x

Hi all,
We've decided to shoehorn another Mocksted in before the end of term. We're not going to tell you when it is, you'll just have to be prepared. It could be Monday but it could be in two weeks. You just won't know. Unless you're a friend of one of the SLT. Obvs.
Thanks x

Hi all,
Please remember that all staff and students should be walking to the left in corridors and on staircases. This is because Boy Jayden is right handed and likes to punch people as they walk past.
Thanks x

Hi all,
Now that Year 11 have left, we've decided to share out "gained time" so that teachers who didn't have Year 11 this year can have some extra planning time. It looks like you'll all be covering 9Z lessons, too since their form tutor has had yet another break down.
Thanks x

Hi teachers of 9Z,
I'm going through your nominations for Awards Evening and I'm surprised to see that Sara (without an H) has been chosen to receive 5 subject prizes. It may have slipped your attention that her family moved to Australia in March and took her with them.
Thanks x

Hi all,
You may have noticed that Colin in 9Z is now identifying as a Giant Panda. I don't know why you are all making such a big deal about it. It's no more unrealistic and far-fetched than most of you claiming to be good teachers.
Thanks x

Hi all,
You may have heard that our CEO, Lord Farquhar of Fark Hall, has been incarcerated again for insider dealing. This means that the guest speaker at our Awards Evening next week will be Tina or Janice. At least we know it will finish before Love Island starts now.
Thanks x

Hi all,

Can someone please tell the Exam Invigilators that our GCSE exams have now finished? The poor old duffers spent all day yesterday wandering up and down the hall, clutching lined paper, trying to avoid the Year 7s who were playing badminton in their PE lesson.
Thanks x

Hi all,

The Year 11 Prom was a huge success. Thanks to the Year 11 tutors for organising the event and having the good sense to stay away. The "Awards Ceremony" was a highlight, with Chantelle winning "Person most likely to gatecrash the Prom" for the third year running.
Thanks x

Hi all,

Don't forget that today is Year 6 Induction Day. We expect each Department to put on all-singing and all-dancing Ofsted "outstanding" lessons which will be filmed for our YouTube channel and our website and used against you in next year's Appraisal.
Thanks x

Hi all,

It's still not too late to go part time next term. If you fancy dropping a day or two, losing a couple of days' pay, yet still seeming to put in 50 hours a week, please let us know. Otherwise we'll have to let some of you go. Tina.
Thanks x

Hi all,
Due to Mrs Johnson's early retirement, we have a vacancy for another Assistant Assistant Vice Assistant Principal's Vice Assistant. This time it's Manager for Improving Lesson Feedback. If you see yourself as the next Academy MILF, talk to Carole in reception. Thanks x

Hi all,
There has been another spelling error in the Staff Newsletter. From September you will each get 3 PPAs per week, not 3 IPAs. The Science Department doesn't need to order that new fridge now. Thanks x

Hi all,
After watching Carry On At Your Convenience on an old DVD in their Business Studies lessons, 9Z have now formed their own union. They are currently in discussions with Head of Year 9 Mr Johnson, arguing for less homework, more holidays and an on-site crèche. Thanks x

Hi all,
You may have noticed that the demountable classrooms have been removed. Apologies to Mrs Johnson who was teaching in there at the time. We aren't getting a new building, we just forgot to renew the lease. History lessons will be outside until further notice. Thanks x

Hi all,
Due to an outbreak of typhoid in The Academy, we will no longer be allowing pupils to refill their water bottles from the old horse trough in the yard. However, 9Z can still sell water in used Prime bottles for £3 at break and lunch "cos you can't prove nuffin".
Thanks x

Hi all,
We would like to confirm that water bottles are permitted in lessons but they must contain only water. Samples taken last week contained vodka, gin, MDMA, and tequila. Heaven knows what we would have found if we had tested the pupils' bottles.
Thanks x

Hi all,
The IT guys have created our new prospectus and it's on our website. Before you ask, you won't recognise any of the staff, pupils or buildings as they've all been created using AI. Well, we wouldn't attract many kids with photos of 9Z, Tina or Janice, would we?
Thanks x

Hi all,
Now that the outdoor temperature is regularly in the 30s and indoor temperatures are pushing 40 degrees we have decided it's a good time to have a crackdown on uniform standards. Top buttons must be fastened, ties knotted properly and blazers worn at all times.
Thanks x

Hi all,

We have finalised the end of term reward trips: Year 7 are going to have a picnic at the beach. Year 8 are going to the cinema then bowling. Year 9 are off to Chessington World of Adventures. Year 10 have GCSE catch up classes. 9Z will be vaping and drinking cider in the park

Thanks x

Hi all,

Yesterday's meeting with our SIP went really well. She made 3 general recommendations: 1) Planning needs to include more differentiation, 2) Low level behaviour must be challenged, 3) 9Z should never be left unsupervised with a hosepipe when there is a SIP visit.

Thanks x

Hi all,

Please be extremely careful operating the electric fans in your classrooms. We don't need any more accidents. So far this week 3 pupils have lost fingertips, Boy Jayden has lost the tip of his tongue and Colin's family have cancelled his circumcision appointment.

Thanks x

Hi all,

Many of you have been asking when next year's teaching timetables will be distributed. The really funny thing is, almost all of the people who have asked won't even be here in September!

Thanks x

Hi all,

There's another spelling mistake in last week's newsletter. The article about Mr Johnson not returning to The Academy as he is permanently living in pain, should have read, "he is permanently living in Spain". Please ask pupils to stop raising money for him.

Thanks x

Hi all,

I know that some of our students are struggling with their personal hygiene at the moment, particularly in this hot weather, but standing in your doorway spraying them with a liberal coating of Lynx Africa is doing nothing for their self-esteem or their asthma.

Thanks x

Hi all,

We have realised that we haven't done enough CPD sessions to complete our 1265 hours. So, we have decided that we'll do one twilight session a week between now and the end of term. There are still 4 parents' evenings, too. You certainly won't be getting bored.

Thanks x

Hi all,

If anyone can remember how to change The Academy bell timer from BST to GMT, can you please get in touch with the Site Team as he has forgotten. If this problem can't be rectified, registration will be at 7:40am tomorrow.

Thanks x

Hi all,
The Health and Beauty department have launched a competition to try to find a better advertising slogan for their "community salon". Apparently, "Don't worry, it'll probably grow back" is putting some people off.
Thanks x

Hi all,
Rewards trips are the penultimate week of term. Pupils with the most positive points get first choice. We are telling you because if you don't want to spend a day at Thorpe Park with 9Z, you'd better start dishing out thousands of points to the nice kids now.
Thanks x

Hi all,
We have discovered that the new supply teacher who has been keeping 9Z calm and well-behaved has been topping up Glade Plug Ins with chloroform in their classroom. Although we think this behaviour is abhorrent, we have extended his contract until the end of July.
Thanks x

Hi all,
The Staff Handbook states that "teaching and support staff should wear professional business attire at all times". Some of you are arriving to work dressed as if your profession is one that goes on down the docks after the pubs close. So, smarten yourselves up.
Thanks x

Hi all,

The Year 11 Year Book is finally finished. It costs £5.99 and is available from the Main Office, the Year 11 office, and can be seen on the top shelf of the local newsagents.

Thanks x

Hi all,

Now that Year 11 have left The Academy, you've no excuses for not doing all of the jobs you've been putting off this year. New schemes of work, Departmental Handbooks and daily risk assessments are due in on Monday and the ceilings in MFL need a lick of paint.

Thanks x

Hi all,

We are having a fire drill this afternoon at 2pm. Yes, we know there are Science GCSEs on at the same time but it is on the calendar. The year 11s can ignore the alarm and carry on. The caretaker is going to block up the bell in the Main Hall with some old socks.

Thanks x

Hi all,

This week's book looks are focusing on Written Teacher Feedback in EAL pupils' books. We expect to see full paragraphs of WWW and EBI with student responses in full sentences in green ink, even though they can't understand English very well. It's Academy policy.

Thanks x

Hi all,
Please congratulate Tina and Janice, who, from September, have been appointed PSHE leads with special responsibility for contraception education. Well, if the cap fits...
Thanks x

Hi all,
If you're leaving The Academy at the end of the Academic Year and intend to give a speech at our final staff briefing, your script must be checked by HR. Send them your final draft before noon this Friday. Remember, it's 15 seconds for each year you've been here.
Thanks x

Hi all,
Now that the Year 11 pupils have left we will be monitoring how you spend your gained time. This is not extra PPA. Most of you will be used to sand the gym floor before we get the Art Department to varnish it. Bring some old clothes, a mask and some sandpaper.
Thanks x

Hi all,
Just to confirm The Academy does not have an official TikTok account, it is a fake, and we are definitely not hosting an Old Folks Nudists' Barbecue on Friday lunchtime or any other lunchtime.
Thanks x

Hi all,
We have just realised that we have double booked the main hall with the French listening GCSE Exams and the Year 6 Open Day. After a meeting lasting almost 30 seconds, our Head of MFL, Mr Andrew, has agreed that the Year 6 pupils can sit quietly at the back.
Thanks x

Hi all,
Some of you have noticed that most of our classrooms have been fitted with CCTV cameras during half term. This is for your safety and in no way will we be monitoring your performance or behaviour, although you may notice a flashing red light during some lessons.
Thanks x

Hi all,
Another week of GCSE exams. The heating has been on all weekend in the Main Hall and the air con has been on all weekend in the gym. Also now that our PGCE students have left, we have no invigilators, so we're using your gained time for this. Check the timetable.
Thanks x

Hi all,
Don't forget, June is Pride Month. There'll be lots of activities going on in The Academy, including special Pride Assemblies from the LGBTQI+ group, rainbow cakes in the canteen, and accidentally outing some members of staff without their knowledge or consent.
Thanks x

Hi all,
Due to "burnout" (laziness, more like), we are looking to appoint two more Associate Assistant Vice Assistant Principals for September. There's no extra money but you won't have a tutor group, thus freeing up an hour a week to do an extra 45 hours work.
Thanks x

Hi all,
Don't forget that reports for all years are due by 6am on Monday. I hope you've all remembered to use the new template we emailed out last night. If not, you're going to have a busy weekend, what with Monday's Mocksted as well.
Thanks x

Hi all,
Tuesday's Year 8 Parents' Evening is Directed Time. If you don't teach Year 8, you are expected to be on site from 5pm until it finishes at 9pm. Your line manager will find you suitably tedious tasks to do which are definitely not in your job description.
Thanks x

Hi all,
Apparently, it's "unfair" that the kids who have long term medical issues won't be allowed on the 100% Attendance Theme Park trip. I think some of you have misunderstood the term "100% Attendance". They'll just have to stay in school with the really naughty kids.
Thanks x

Hi all,
For Monday's twilight CPD, we have invited a guest speaker, who is going to explain his Assessment Research in Secondary Education thesis for us. Please be in the Main Hall at 3:20 as Mr Shackleton is going to talk though his ARSE from 3:30 until 7pm.
Thanks x

Hi all,
Janice informs me that Monday is the final day to pay your £10 deposit for the Christmas Staff Do at The Greasy Ferret on the otherwise abandoned industrial estate. If you're in the Humanities, Drama or Music departments, I'd not bother.
Thanks x

Hi form tutors,
I'm taking sealed bids on the tutor groups you'd like for September. Cash only. Used 10s or 20s and definitely non-sequential notes. Consideration will be given to serious bids only.
Thanks x

Hi all,
Now that Year 11 have left, we're changing break duties. Year 7 and 8 teams will be inside, policing the canteen. Years 10 and 11 are outside supervising the fights on the back field, and Year 9 will take up sniper positions on the roof of the Main Building.
Thanks x

Hi all,
Just to let you know that the electric car charging points by The Academy Senior Staff Entrance are for the sole use of staff of Vice Principal level and higher. They are for The Academy's fleet of Teslas. Can you please stop charging your milk float there, Tina?
Thanks x

Hi all,
Please remember that we have nothing against anyone having babies and taking "maternity leave" but you must be aware that all planned absences require staff to set "meaningful cover work" for all of their classes. Read your terms of employment, Sophie.
Thanks x

Hi all,
We would like to apologise to anyone who was traumatised by 9Z's Astronomy Club assembly on Friday morning. They should never have been allowed to show their video, "Is there life on Uranus?" As a result we have had to re-varnish the floor of the Main Hall.
Thanks x

Hi all,
After half term you'll notice we have installed metal detectors in the Academy's entrances and fire exits. We are not worried about students arriving with weapons, we are concerned about which staff are stealing teapots and teaspoons from communal break rooms.
Thanks x

Hi all,

We have noticed that some of you have set "out of office" replies to your Academy emails. If this is you, please switch this off and re-read your contract of employment (page 1347, chapter 12, paragraph 63, subsection 4: availability). Enjoy the half term break.

Thanks x

Hi all,

We have a Cover Supervisor vacancy. They'll be expected to work full time in the Maths Department as a full time maths teacher, planning and delivering lessons to bottom sets from Years 7 - 11. The salary is £21000, but pro rata as you won't be paid for holidays.

Thanks x

Hi all,

We have changed the criteria for Prom. Pupils no longer need 80% attendance, fewer than 30 detentions, and no exclusions. We no longer care what they got in their mocks. Only two kids are eligible and it's costing us a fortune. So, anyone can go and bring a mate.

Thanks x

Hi all,

Under no circumstances must you allow students to remove their pullovers in The Academy. Ms Turner, in MFL, let 9Z remove their pullovers because they said it was "too hot" and the stench was overpowering. Doctors say her sense of smell will most likely never come back.

Thanks x

Hi all,

We have written a new writing policy to go alongside our literacy policy. The Writing, Teaching and Assessment and Feedback policy is just 240 pages long. You must read it and sign the Google Form to prove you have done this. It's on the VLE under WTAF.

Thanks x

Hi all,

The Trust has high standards for its teaching staff and has decreed that, from September, if you didn't get a 1st in your degree, or got a degree in an easy subject like Dance or Art, you'll no longer be allowed to work for the Academy. Unless you're SLT. Obvs.

Thanks x

Hi all,

The SLT wants to thank you all for your continued hard work and to wish you all a relaxing half term. Also don't forget that end of year reports are due on June 5th. This year you have to write reports for the pupils you don't teach, too. It's a pastoral thing.

Thanks x

Hi all,

There has been another error in the latest Options Booklet: "GCSE Fart classes" should read "GCSE Art classes". At least we hope it should. Please make your Year 9 groups aware of this. 9Z will be devastated.

Thanks x

Hi all,
Please be aware that our social medias have been hacked again. Despite the rumours, we are definitely not replacing the traditional TWAT Leavers' Hoodies with TWAT Leavers' Tattoos this year. They will both be available.
Thanks x

Hi all,
We have a vacancy for a TA to work with 9Z from September. The ideal candidate must have HLTA Level 4 qualification, a calm and pleasant disposition, a sense of humour, nerves of steel and a karate black belt with twelfth dan.
Thanks x

Hi all,
When we said that pupils could play on the field at lunchtimes, we meant the sports field at the side of The Academy, not the Territorial Army's Live Ammo Training Field around the back. Luckily, there were no casualties and 9Z only found a few live grenades.
Thanks x

Hi all,
Just a reminder that The Academy Tie is an important and compulsory part of our uniform and must be worn by all students at all times. It's never too hot to wear a tie! Nobody wears two ties when it's really cold, do they? 9Z are exempt from this rule. Obviously.
Thanks x

Hi all,

From September Mr Frobisher will be taking over as Literacy Coordinator. He's probably not qualified for the job but he looks the part with his weedy frame, greasy hair and his thick glasses.

Thanks x

Hi all,

We are having, yet again, to rethink our Make Up and Jewellery Policy. This morning one of Chantelle's eye lashes got caught in the library door and it took three firemen and two paramedics to get her free. Chantelle will be OK but the eye lash didn't make it.

Thanks x

Hi all,

It's another week of GCSE exams here in The Academy. The temperature in the hall is currently 40 degrees centigrade, the windows are painted shut, the fire doors are padlocked and there's 8 wasps in there. We hope pupils have revised enough to get their targets.

Thanks x

Hi all,

We've updated the handbook with our new "Wasp in the Classroom Policy". Please make sure that you read the 16 relevant chapters and write a risk assessment for every room you teach in. We will test this by randomly releasing bees and wasps during the school day.

Thanks x

Hi all,
We know that some of you are struggling with the cost of living crisis at the moment and so we have decided that we will freeze next term's parking charges for the staff car park. We're even going to make weekend parking half price for GCSE revision lessons.
Thanks x

Hi all,
During yesterday's Book Looks we noticed that some books had pages missing. On Monday, every child will go through their exercise books in every subject and number the pages. Anyone with missing pages will be given detention for destroying Academy property.
Thanks x

Hi all,
The last Monday in May seems like the ideal time to have a crackdown on uniform standards. Anyone not complying with our strict uniform policy (which we've never enforced) will be sent home to change first thing. Tutors will police this and contact parents.
Thanks x

Hi all,
Just a reminder about The Academy's Staff Dress Code. The wearing of open-toed footwear is not permitted under any circumstances. Nobody needs to see your fungal infections and some of our KS3 pupils are still having nightmares about Janice's extra toe.
Thanks x

Hi all,
Mrs Stevens has recruited some of our Year 10 BTEC students to mentor their peers and be her Vocational Project Leaders. Keep a look out for her VPL in this morning's assembly.
Thanks x

Hi all,
You only have 13 days left to hand in your notice if you intend to leave The Academy at the end of this Academic Year. You don't even need to write a letter as we have posted a Google Form link on the VLE. We've already filled in forms for all the MFL Department.
Thanks x

Hi all,
From September you will be required to use an Official Academy Planner. There's a page for every lesson, a page for feedback and self reflection on lessons, as well as a section for your line manager to complete each day. The A5 version weighs around 15 kilos.
Thanks x

Hi all,
Tomorrow, we will be sending out the options lists to all Heads of Department. If you see anyone on there who you don't think will be able to manage in your subject area or who might misbehave, let me know straight away and we'll make them do History or French.
Thanks x

Hi all,

I have been asked by the cleaners to point out that the new toilet brushes in the staff toilets are there to clean the toilets when you have finished. They are not supposed to be used as an alternative to toilet paper.

Thanks x

Hi Music Department,

Can you please make sure that when you are rehearsing with the choir for the end of year concert, that all the windows are closed. We've had complaints about the noise from the abattoir next door.

Thanks x

Hi all,

To save money we will no longer be giving new exercise books to students who fill their books, from now until September. They can work on paper. Also, next week we will be having book scrutinies in all subjects. Make sure they're perfectly presented and marked.

Thanks x

Hi all,

Tomorrow's twilight CPD is the one we had to postpone from September so that our CEO could rant about exam results for four hours. So, meet in the Main Hall at 4pm for "Ice Breakers - Getting To Know Our New Staff". Actually almost all of them have left.

Thanks x

Hi all,
We saw a couple of you bragging on social media that you had finished your end of year reports. Therefore, we have decided to change the format. This year's reports will have new comment banks, will be A5 booklets, and we have disabled the "copy and paste" tool.
Thanks x

Hi all,
We are looking for a new Staff Governor. Angela kept asking questions and coming up with good ideas, so we decided the job was not for her. We gave her more teaching responsibility, put her on a support plan, and told her she should step down. Works every time.
Thanks x

Hi all,
We are looking for two new SLT members to micro manage our Heads of Department. The title of the positions: Assistant Senior Specialist Heads Overseeing Less Experienced Staff. If you see yourself as one of our new ASSHOLES, please see Carol in the office.
Thanks x

Hi all,
For no reason at all, other than our obsession with micro-management, we will scrutinise all staff planners on Monday. You must leave them at the office before 7:15am. We expect to see full lesson plans for every lesson this year. You'll get them back on Friday.
Thanks x

Hi all,
It was great to see so many of you getting involved and quite vocal in this morning's 7:30am sims training. For future reference, BYOD stands for Bring Your Own Device, not Bring Your Own Drinks.
Thanks x

Hi all,
Mr Martin informs me that The Willows Academy First 11 won their first match of the season yesterday with a record breaking win against St Michael's. This would be amazing news if St Michael's was a school and not the residential care home around the corner. Still, they all count.
Thanks x

Hi all,
After the exchange with a school in Burundi, the pupils, seeing their partners living in poverty, poor health and poor housing, raised some money and bought each family a goat. I'm not sure where our pupils are going to keep the goats but it was a lovely gesture.
Thanks x

Hi all,
As this is Healthy Schools Week, we have decided to ban all sugary snacks, crisps, and fizzy drinks. Please search your tutees' bags during registration and bring all contraband to my office straight away. Give any offenders a one hour detention. With you. Obvs.
Thanks x

Hi all,

Can we please make sure that we are on duty promptly at break times. Today there was a very unpleasant incident when Shanice from Year 10 may or may not have looked at Chantelle. Luckily they both had their phones so didn't fight, just dissed each other on Instagram.

Thanks x

Hi all,

To show our appreciation for all the hard work you do, we are going to get the pupils to clap for two minutes during each assembly. This will be instead of any pay rises over the next year. It seemed to work for the nurses.

Thanks x

Hi all,

Just one more exclusion will trigger another Ofsted inspection, so can you please start to be more lenient to our less-than-cooperative pupils. Turn a deaf ear to their swearing, a blind eye to the violence and theft and we'll all be OK for the rest of the year.

Thanks x

Hi all,

Today's canteen special is not, as advertised, Coronation Chicken, but chlorinated chicken. I don't suppose any of the pupils will notice. They fill up on Doritos, Monster and Red Bull at break time and are usually still on the ceiling at lunch time.

Thanks x

Hi all,

We are revising our rewards system. Here is the list of when points can be awarded:

- Good class/homework 1 point
- Good exam results 3 points
- Good coursework 3 points
- After hours club 2 points
- Representing the school 2 points
- 9Z following any expectation 500 points

Thanks x

Hi all,

As we care about your Well-Being and Work Life Balance, we have decided that, from September, you will no longer be required to respond to any Academy emails between the hours of midnight and 5:30am. At weekends. Unless it's marked URGENT. Obviously.

Thanks x

Hi all,

The extra bank holiday means you won't reach your 1265 contracted hours. So we've decided to give you a choice of an extra day's teaching or a full day's CPD. They will both be on the 24th of July. I hope you haven't booked any holidays for then.

Thanks x

Hi all,

Because you'll all have had an extra day off to prepare, we have decided to move Thursday's Mocksted to Tuesday. We will open The Academy 10 minutes earlier so you can do your photocopying. Although the engineer won't have been and fixed the problem by then. Thanks x

Hi all,

We have had our IT guys studying the footage of the Coronation procession, looking for any of you, who phoned in sick yesterday, in the crowds. There'll be some "two minute conversations" on Tuesday. You're not fooling anyone in that Camilla mask, Mrs Hampson. Thanks x

Hi all,

Year 11 students start Study Leave next Friday. Here is the plan:
- 9:00 Arrive at school drunk (them, not us)
- 9:15 Assembly and photos
- 11:00 Shirt signing and goodbyes
- 12 noon: leave premises
- 12:15 Wetherspoons
- 15:00 Return to the Academy to cause trouble

Thanks x

Hi all,

We feel we need to explain that Year 7 pupil, Clarissa Johnson's article in the latest Pupil Newsletter entitled "Charles and Camilla have mange and diarrhoea" was, in fact, an update on the health of her gerbils and nothing to do with our wonderful royal family.

Thanks x

Hi all,

New format seating plans must be uploaded to the VLE before 4pm today. They must include: name of pupil, PP, EAL, FSM, EVER6, SEND, current level, old level, end of year target, End of KS target, GCSE Target, A level target, favourite cheese and a colour photo.

Thanks x

Hi all,

We are rethinking our policy of forcing you to use De Bono's Thinking Hats in every lesson. Almost every child in Key Stage 3 has caught nits and all of the Geography Department have ringworm.

Thanks x

Hi all,

Just to let you know that the big hole in the back fence has now been fixed. This means that 9Z can't escape at lunchtime to get chips, Mr Johnson can't go to The Nag's Head and Chantelle has had to reschedule her hair and nails appointment on Friday afternoon.

Thanks x

Hi all,

Thursday is our Open Evening. From 4pm until 10:30 you will all be expected to be on the premises, in departments, grovelling and fawning to prospective Year 7 pupils for next year. Anyone caught saying anything negative will get 9Z for a tutor group next year.
Thanks x

Hi all,

We have been asked to do a thorough analysis of our Value Added Grades In National Assessments. Please make sure that all of your most recent VAGINA data is uploaded to the VLE , ready to be inspected by the end of school tonight.
Thanks x

Hi all,

Remember that we don't allow staff to take time off for medical appointments during the school day. I'm pretty sure that hospitals, doctors and dentists are open in the holidays and after 3:30pm on weekdays. Quite frankly some of you are just having a laugh.
Thanks x

Hi all,

Sadly, we have failed to achieve Healthy Schools Status. We thought we had it nailed this time but it seems that selling fruit flavoured vapes in the tuck shop is a no-no. To get around this we have created our own award, which our CEO will award us next week.
Thanks x

Hi all,
Just a couple of reminders to those who are considering striking tomorrow: 1) it's not worth the grief we'll give you for it, 2) you will lose your parking space, 3) you will not have a classroom in September (if you're still here)
Thanks x

Hi all,
The final date for ordering exercise books for next year is tomorrow. Make sure you order three for each student: one for use in class, one for best work and one for Ofsted, which only you will write in using your left hand.
Thanks x

Hi all,
Recent Learning Walks have shown us that some of you are lacking enthusiasm for your subjects, so, in Tuesday's Twilight CPD, we will be teaching you how to appear more enthusiastic. Our guest speaker is a Kriss Akabusi impersonator, the real one was unavailable.
Thanks x

Hi all,
As you are probably aware, to free up some space, we no longer use our old VLE in The Academy and have deleted all your accounts and passwords. Let's hope there was nothing important on there.
Admittedly, we probably should have told you before we deleted it.
Thanks x

Hi all,

Just to let you know that Chantelle has been prescribed some new medication. As with any medication we have been told there will be some side effects. You may notice some extreme changes in her behaviour at first. At times, she may appear calm, polite and compliant.

Thanks x

Hi all,

Don't forget that all Year 11 coursework for all subjects is due by 6:30am on Tuesday. Any student who still has work to complete must have it finished this weekend. This is your responsibility. You can get their addresses from sims.

Thanks x

Hi all,

Yesterday was the final Appraisal meetings of the current cycle. Anyone who was taking strike action yesterday and missed their meeting has failed. Anyone who was hoping to apply for UPS can reapply next year. If they're still here.

Thanks x

Hi all,

Today is GCSE Speaking Exams Day. It is also the Regional KS3 Tap Dancing Festival, building work starts on the new underground car park foundations, there will be fire drills during lessons 2 and 4 and we're also hosting the World Lawn Mowing Championships.

Thanks x

Hi all,

With the Year 11 students leaving soon, we will soon be recruiting Year 10s to become our Academy Senior Students. The duties of an ASS include: lording it over the smaller kids, and generally being unpleasant and thinking they're better than everyone else.

Thanks x

Hi all,

Don't forget that, even though Monday is a Bank Holiday, we are still opening The Academy for lessons for KS4 intervention and revision groups in all subjects, from 7am. A lot of pupils will turn up as they need to have 150 attendance stamps to get a prom ticket.

Thanks

Hi all,

The Music Department is holding auditions for their Summer Production tomorrow after school. Remember, no KS4 students will be allowed to perform because of exams, and only Disadvantaged Students are allowed to audition for main roles because of Academy Quotas.

Thanks x

Hi all,

During our recent Learning Walks, it was noted that some of you keep going "off script" when speaking to pupils. Remember, that when reprimanding a student, if they don't say the official warning along with you in a sarcastic voice, then you're doing it wrong.

Thanks x

Hi all,

We are looking for, yet another, charismatic, blue-suited, brown loafer-shod future leader to take the role of Head of Assessment, Numeracy and Data. If you think you're experienced enough and ready for an Academy HAND job, please see Carole in the office.

Thanks x

Hi all,

Due to a spelling error in one of our latest job adverts, we have had several applications impressing us with their extensive knowledge of installing kitchens, bathrooms and bedrooms. Ideally, we really need a Head of MFL though, not Head of MFI.

Thanks x

Hi all,

There will be minibus training for all Year 11 tutors tomorrow. When the GCSE exams start you will be responsible for making sure your pupils attend their exams on time. You will go to their houses at 8 am and force them to attend.

Thanks x

Hi all,

Tutors make sure that pupils are adhering to our jewellery policy. No jewellery is allowed apart from one stud in each ear and a watch. Any child not conforming will get a 1 hour same day detention with you. You'll also have to deal with any stroppy parents.

Thanks x

Hi all,

From tomorrow the Daily Staff Briefing will be videoed and shared with all staff on the VLE. If you are on duty and unable to make Briefing, you must watch the video in your own time and complete the quiz on Google Forms within 24 hours.

Thanks x

Hi all,

The new Duty Team Schedule is on the VLE, TEAMS, and a post it on the staffroom kettle, so you've no excuse for not being in the correct place. You must be in position within 5 seconds of the bell but must not release any groups early. We teach to the bell here.

Thanks x

Hi all,

Monday is the final day for ordering a Year 11 Leavers' Hoodie. The Pastoral Team will then scour all of the students' requested nicknames for anything rude, untoward or offensive. We cannot have any smut on them underneath the great name, TWAT.

Thanks x

Hi all,

We are delighted to announce our newest member of the SLT, Mr Raab. He starts on Monday as Assistant Principal In Charge of Appraisal, Well-Being and Staff Morale. He has amazing references.

Thanks x

Hi all,
Can we please check the spelling of all articles which you submit for the pupils' newsletter? This week's feature from Food Tech which read, "we could smell the delicious aroma of Year 9's panties all around the school", should have read "pasties". We're really sorry.
Thanks x

Hi all,
Can we please stop giving positive behaviour points to naughty children who behave for 5 minutes? They can be used in The Academy shop and you're bankrupting us. Boy Jayden has enough points now to get a BMW M3 and Chantelle has enough for a villa in Tuscany. Thanks x

Hi all,
Remember that this week's Compulsory Staff Well-Being 2 Hour Yoga Class starts at 6:30am on Friday in the gym. Could there be a better way to start a Mocksted Day?
Thanks x

Hi all,
In preparation for Friday's Mocksted can you please make sure that all work is marked up to date and that there is personalised feedback for every assessment for every child. Failing that just tear out the pages that aren't marked. Like English do.
Thanks x

Hi all,

There have been complaints at how intensely we've been inspecting departments, so we've made a new scale:

1. the dipping of the toe
2. the quick paddle
3. the "up to the knees"
4. he pleasant swim
5. the Deep Dive
6. the fight to the death with a Kraken

Thanks x

Hi all,

There has been an overwhelming response from children and staff wishing to go on The Academy's Ski Trip. We never realised how many of our pupils would be so interested in a visit to a yoghurt factory.

Thanks x

Hi all,

The local council's Sex Ed Team will be in The Academy today with their "Bonk Bus", giving out relationship advice and free condoms. Be prepared for a day of water bombs, balloon animals and KS3 suffocations. I imagine some of the kids will misbehave with them, too.

Thanks x

Hi all,

This week's Pupil Voice questionnaire will be just for EAL students. There are about 400 questions which require answers in full sentences. Please send all your EAL kids to the library at break. Fifteen minutes should be more than enough for them to fill it in.

Thanks x

Hi all,

Last night's CPD on marking and feedback went really well. Huge thanks to the T&L Team who showed us PowerPoints they had downloaded but hadn't read and played us videos which they hadn't watched, especially the one dubbed into Portuguese with Greek subtitles.

Thanks x

Hi all,

Today we welcome our new governor, Mr Johnson, to The Academy. He is the link Governor of Business Studies, History, IT, and English. He's very keen and hopefully will be a much better GOBSHITE than his predecessor.

Thanks x

Hi all,

Can we please keep an eye on behaviour in the bus queues. Today there were complaints about pushing, shouting, swearing and spitting. Quite frankly, the children were horrified by some of your behaviour.

Thanks x

Hi all,
To eradicate internal truancy at The Academy, we have decided not to give timetables to the students. From today, they can just turn up to whatever lesson they fancy. Be prepared to have mixed year groups and differentiate as best you can for them all.
Thanks x

Hi all,
Now that the weather is getting warmer, a quick reminder that rolled up skirts and knotted blouses tied above the navel are not permitted in The Academy. This rule applies to the kids, too.
Thanks x

Hi all,
On Wednesday we have a professional make up artist visiting The Academy. She'll be spending the afternoon demonstrating her "little is best" subtlety and application techniques. This is for all Year 9 and 10 girls, the Head of English and the NQT in maths.
Thanks x

Hi all,
We could be in for a boost to our budgets from Monday. Our bursar, Mr Johnson, has put all of next term's budgets on a horse called Norfolk Enchants in today's Grand National. We can't lose. He says.
Thanks x

Hi all,
Our best wishes go out to Mr Johnson who was rushed to hospital last night after collapsing at home. Apparently, he has done so many Deep Dives this week, he has been diagnosed with Decompression Sickness.
Thanks x

Hi all,
Here's a reminder of the system for ordering supplies:
    1) Complete the 9 preorder forms on the VLE
    2) Check there's enough money in your budget
    3) Wait 4 to 6 weeks for the items to be approved
    4) Go to Staples and just buy the stuff yourself
Thanks x

Hi all,
Thank you for making our visitors so welcome, yesterday. We were expecting Ofsted. They had just come to pick up their grandson for a medical appointment. It's a mistake anyone could have made.
Thanks x

Hi all,
Our Teacher Buddy Scheme is working well. We have paired up some new staff with more experienced, reliable staff. They share problems and views about The Academy. The new staff then tell SLT, who start capability proceedings against the more expensive colleague.
Thanks x

Hi all,

For Monday's CPD day we will have a full morning of ice breakers, VAK, Maslow, Bloom's and Hooks' Taxonomy and an afternoon of queuing for the photocopier. Heads of Year will be babysitting the kids who forgot it was a CPD day.

Thanks x

Hi all,

We've changed the requirements for a Prom Ticket. Students will be allowed to go to Prom even if they don't meet any of the criteria published in April. As long as they apologise to the Head of Year whilst staring at their shoes so as not to laugh, they'll be OK.

Thanks x

Hi all,

As a part of our modernisation drive we have decided to get rid of The Academy's old Library. Unwelcoming, smelling of mould, tatty, dark, creepy, damp and just downright unpleasant, the librarian, Mrs Johnson will be sadly missed.

Thanks x

Hi all,

To save time with marking and feedback, we are going to start to use Whole Class Feedback sheets. There is a sample on the VLE for you to adapt. Make sure that each pupil is given their own Whole Class Feedback sheet with their name and personal targets on it.

Thanks x

Hi all,

Due to an increase in complaints against teachers, we have decided that you should all wear body-cams during lessons. This will improve behaviour and also stop the need for SLT to do lesson observations or learning walks. You can get them on Amazon for about £40.

Thanks x

Hi all,

Due to high utilities costs, we're having an economy drive. All heaters will be removed from classrooms, toilets are only to be flushed in an emergency, lights are only to be on when it has actually gone dark, and the library is just going to stock braille books.

Thanks x

Hi all,

Please check that pupils have the correct shoes after PE lessons. We've had complaints about kids going home in the wrong shoes. Also, can you check that PE staff have the correct shoes. Mr Johnson was walking round in circles all day with two left Nikes on.

Thanks x

Hi all,

Due to the ceiling collapsing in Remove, we're having a change of venue for the naughty pupils, as it is totally unsafe. From tomorrow they will be based in the staff room. Feel free to spend your breaks in Remove. It's not safe for kids but it's OK for teachers.

Thanks x

Hi all,
Just a reminder that, if you are considering leaving The Academy at Christmas, you only have a couple of weeks to hand in your notice. Some of you should really give some serious thought to this. You're not enjoying it and we have a long waiting list of ECTs.
Thanks x

Hi all,
Just to let you know that, if you were hoping to buy a poppy, we are waiting for another batch of poppies to arrive from the British Legion. 9Z bought the entire supply, thinking they could harvest some opium from them.
Thanks x

Hi all,
We are trying to get a Healthy Schools Award for The Academy and, starting today, the canteen will serve every student their 5 fruit and veg a day. At lunch, each pupil will be given a potato, three sprouts and a banana.
Thanks x

Hi all,
After much thought we have decided to stop putting a red dot on our PP students' exercise books. The main reason is that every time Boy Jayden was given his maths book, he saw the red dot and thought he was being targeted by a sniper on the bike shed roof.
Thanks x

Hi all,
When out on duty at the end of the day, can you please make sure that you have on your Academy Hi Viz jacket. Parents have complained they don't know who the staff are and so don't know who to complain to or shout abuse at.
Thanks x

Hi all,
After several complaints from all of the teaching unions, we have agreed to stop including GCSE exam results as an Appraisal Target. So, this year you only need to pass 14 of your 15 targets. Anyone with a TLR will only have to pass 19 out of 20.
Thanks x

Hi all,
After a number of visits to a doctor and a behaviour specialist, it has been decided that Tom and Paul can use fidget toys in lessons. The rest of the PE department is still waiting to be assessed.
Thanks x

Hi all,
We hope you're enjoying the half term break and spending some quality time with loved ones, rewriting those Schemes of Work, planning lessons and drawing those Learning Journeys? See you all tomorrow for GCSE Revision. Well, not me. Obvs. I'm in the Seychelles.
Thanks x

Hi all,
Miss Johnson is leaving us after half term to take up a job as a circus acrobat. Apparently, she's looking forward to having fewer hoops to jump through than the teachers at The Academy applying for UPS.
Thanks x

Hi all,
Don't forget that if you fail your Appraisal, you can appeal. We have an independent panel, made up of our CEO, Bursar, and Chair of Governor's, who will scrutinise any appeal, and feed back to you on why they agree with the original decision within 48 hours.
Thanks x

Hi all,
Please remember, that if you are coming into The Academy this week, you are responsible for providing lunch for your students. Also the heating will be switched off to save money. And so will the electric. And the water, so don't flush the toilets.
Thanks x

Hi all,
There'll be some disruption to The Academy car park for a few weeks. We're installing electric vehicle charging points and building a power station to create the electricity to charge them. The road will be widened to allow access to the trucks delivering coal.
Thanks x

Hi all,

From Monday all KS4 exercise books will be replaced by A4 paper and a lever arch file for each subject. This means that the pupils can still revise while you are marking their work. It will also improve their organisational skills. What could possibly go wrong?

Thanks x

Hi all,

From Monday there'll be a new marking policy. There's a different policy for each subject and each year group, written by an SLT PE teacher who knows nothing about your subject. You can find the new 650 page document on the VLE, somewhere. Apparently.

Thanks x

Hi all,

Don't forget that Year 11 will be doing another set of "surprise mocks" starting on Monday. Also, make sure that you award them at least two full grades below what they actually got. This will motivate them to work even harder for the real exams.

Thanks x

Hi all,

Our social media accounts have been hacked again. The Academy's KS3 Boys' Changing Rooms have not been awarded UNESCO Heritage Site Status and there will not be a special ceremony led by Antonio Guterres on Friday. We wouldn't wish that smell on anybody.

Thanks x

Hi all,
Just a reminder about The Academy Dress Code. Yesterday, Mr Johnson Head of PE, came to an SLT interview dressed in just a T-shirt and very short shorts. This is not really acceptable for an Assistant Headship in The Academy, although we did admire his balls.
Thanks x

Hi all,
The Academy servers will be down for at least the next five days. One of the IT Team appears to have downloaded a virus whilst playing Frogger on a North Korean gaming site. Reports are still due on Monday. It's on The Calendar.
Thanks x

Hi all,
Just a reminder that, to save money, we've cancelled our contract with the refuse collection company. This means you must take all classroom rubbish home and put it in your domestic recycling and rubbish bins. Also can you all take some of "MFL Elvis"'s gin bottles?
Thanks x

Hi all,
If you're not teaching intervention lessons this week, it would be a good time to come in and change your displays. Also, because there are so many students in this week, you're all expected to come in and do your break duties.
Thanks x

Hi all,
Just a reminder that The Academy is in the middle of a residential area and the locals don't need to hear you swearing, screaming, shouting and crying when you leave the premises at 11pm after a CPD session overruns.
Thanks x

Hi all,
We, at The Academy, would like to wish everyone a Happy Easter. You should take some time out today to relax with loved ones (or your families). We've decided this will be between 1:15 and 2pm today. You won't receive any emails or messages during this time.
Thanks x

Hi all,
Remember that tomorrow's GCSE Revision Lessons will be via Zoom only. The Academy will be closed all day on Easter Sunday and reopen for Intervention at 6:30 on Monday morning. Attendance is compulsory for all Year 11 staff. Let's hope some kids turn up, too.
Thanks x

Hi all,
We have had complaints from the PE department about some of you making fun of their intelligence and career choices. I can assure you all that PE is not just "kicking balls", there's sometimes some catching and fetching to do, as well.
Thanks x

Hi all,
There has been yet another spelling mistake in the Staff Bulletin. The second line of our chaplain, Father Johnson's Easter Blessing should have read "Jesus died so that we would be saved from sins" not "sims".
Thanks x

Hi all,
Some of our Junior SLT Members will be in The Academy over the Easter weekend doing book checks. I've already given them a list of which subjects and groups to look at and I've already sent out emails about Support Plans. Happy Easter.
Thanks x

Hi all,
We are going to start Appraisal Catch Ups from Monday via Zoom. We're not going to let a little thing like the holidays get in the way of not giving you a pay rise.
Thanks x

Hi all,
Just a reminder that next year's Schemes of Learning must be submitted to your link SLT before noon on the 16th of April. They must include detailed lesson plans and assessments. We will change the format and the assessment timetable 4 or 5 times before June.
Thanks x

Hi all,

We forgot to send out the new Appraisal paperwork last week, so you're getting it today. Please complete and send it to your line manager by 5 o'clock this afternoon. Meetings will start on Monday.

Thanks x

Hi all,

Our Head of Maths, Miss Johnson, has won an award from the National Office for Research into Knowledge and Statistics. Her NORKS will be on display in The Academy Foyer from Monday.

Thanks x

Hi all,

We are putting together a Working Party to organise planning and delivery of Catch Up lessons for KS4 and need help to organise it. If you'd like to be part of the Catch Up Lessons Team, please email Mr Marrs, CULT@twat.com

Thanks x

Hi all,

There was another error in this week's Staff Bulletin: Our Teaching and Learning Lead, Mrs Johnson, has just published a book, "How To Run A Successful Department In An Academy Trust", not "How To Ruin A Successful Department In An Academy Trust". Sorry, Gemma.

Thanks x

Hi all,
The Academy is closed to all staff next Tuesday as the local Dog Breeders' Association is holding their annual show. Some of you have asked about the smells and faeces in the Main Hall but, don't worry, we've hired a team of cleaners to come in the day before.
Thanks x

Hi all,
If you are in The Academy leading Catch Up or Intervention Lessons this week, remember that you must provide lunch for all the pupils who attend. Make sure you keep any receipts so we can refund you out of your departmental budget... if there's any money left.
Thanks x

Hi all,
We said "Goodbye" to the Geography Department on Friday. If you see any of them over Easter, please don't mention it to them: They may not have picked up their emails yet.
Thanks x

Hi all,
We're sorry that we can't pay you teaching GCSE Revision Lessons in the holidays. The new reception area carpet has cost twice as much as anticipated. We told them we wanted TWAT woven into it but it arrived with photos of our principal's face printed on it.
Thanks x

Hi all,

We were to have had the exterminators in over Easter to get rid of the rodent problem in the canteen. However, we have realised it would be much cheaper and trendier to just rebrand as The Rat Café: Eat lunch with your furry friends.

Thanks x

Hi all,

After losing 5 court cases in as many weeks, we have decided to end the contract with our Legal Advisor, Mr Johnson. He will, however, be staying on in The Academy in a different role in the SLT Lounge. He's a much better barista than he ever was a barrister.

Thanks x

Hi all,

The first day back is Behaviour Training. Our new Behaviour Lead will be showing us how to get on the right side of our more challenging pupils by teaching us current slang, new vaping techniques, and fist-bumping every child as they enter your classroom.

Thanks x

Hi all,

The Academy's social media sites have been hacked again for an April Fool's "joke". We are not having an "Everything Must Go Closing Down Sale" and pupils' uniform is not changing to orange jumpsuits after Easter. It's not until September.

Thanks x

Hi all,

Just wanted to thank you all for your hard work and dedication this term. I hope you can all find time to relax and spend time with loved ones. Don't forget Year 11 intervention lessons all next week and interim reports for all pupils are due on Wednesday.

Thanks x

Hi all,

The staff room Tea and Coffee Club will be starting up again after the Easter Break. If you wish to be considered for membership, you must write a letter of application, stating your intent and provide the names of two referees, who are not friends or relatives.

Thanks x

Hi all,

Tomorrow is not only the final day, but also the final "Book Look" of term. Please ensure that you deliver every child's book on the list for your subject to the Board Room for 7:30am. We want to see their real classwork books, not the ones we show to Ofsted.

Thanks x

Hi all,

Yesterday's KS3 Easter Assembly ended in chaos. Every time the Deputy Assistant Principal, when describing the end of term activities, said, "Mr Johnson's Egg Hunt", all of 9Z shouted, "Yes, he is!"

Thanks x

Hi all,

Remember that this term's data for KS3 is due by 6pm today. We know you've only been given a few hours to complete this and nobody is even going to look at it before next term, but it's on the calendar so you must get it done. Support Plans for any late entries.

Thanks x

Hi all,

The Academy was broken into last night and the contents of the iPad trolley were stolen. Luckily, the insurance company have said they will pay out and Boy Jayden tells us his associates will let us have them back for £10 each. Win win.

Thanks x

Hi all,

Last week's Student of the Week was a close call. It was between Kylie Jones and Boy Jayden. Kylie got top marks in all her exams, her homework was amazing and she raised £300 for charity. Jayden didn't tell anyone to f*** off until Tuesday afternoon, so he wins.

Thanks x

Hi all,

We have just noticed that in the Staff Handbook, it says "all pupils' exercise books are to be deep-marked on a bi-weekly basis". Some of you have taken this to mean "every 2 weeks" whereas it actually means "twice a week". Please sort this out over Easter.

Thanks x

Hi all,
Please do not upload any more photos of yesterday's PE Department Well-Being Bottomless Brunch to the WhatsApp. You'd think at least one of them would be wearing pants.
Thanks x

Hi all,
As we don't know how to change the school bells and have laid off the entire site team to save a few pennies, The Academy teaching day will now start at 9:30am and finish at 4:15pm until October half term. Now we can have Daily Staff CPD Briefings from 8am.
Thanks x

Hi all,
We had The Call on Friday afternoon. Don't worry though, we have uprooted all the local road signs and replaced the board out front with a huge sign that says: The Willows Retirement Village. 9Z are outsourcing grey wigs, pink cardigans and Zimmer frames.
Thanks x

Hi all,
Just 5 days left until the Easter break. That means we've got just enough time to do yet another set of GCSE mock exams before Wednesday's Mocksted, Thursday's Learning Walks and Friday's Book Looks. Mock papers are to be graded and standardised for Wednesday.
Thanks x

Hi all,
Just to let you know that we have failed, yet again, to get Healthy Schools Status. Apparently, it was replacing the canteen with the burger van and the tobacconist's section of the Tuck Shop which did for us this time.
Thanks x

Hi all,
The Academy Library is open for business from Monday! After a great deal of deliberation, Mrs Johnson and her Year 7 librarians have rejected the Dewey Decimal system and just decided to put the big book on the bottom shelf and the little book on the top shelf.
Thanks x

Hi all,
Please question strangers in The Academy, particularly if they do not have a TWAT lanyard. We currently have 28 supply teachers but today some locals nonchalantly signed in at reception and just came in for a warm because the local Wetherspoons was closed.
Thanks x

Hi all,
I've received an email from the local "university" (the former full-of-itself Polytechnic) saying that they will not send us any more PGCE students until we return the ones from last term. If anyone knows where they might be or sees one lying around, let me know.
Thanks x

Hi all,
Please make sure you fill in the Easter GCSE Revision Lessons sheet before the end of term. All Year 11 class teachers must put on at least 2 revision sessions over the two weeks. Sessions should last a minimum of 60 minutes and homework must be set and marked.
Thanks x

Hi all,
When answering the telephone, could we please stop using the acronym and start to use the full name of the Academy. Don't just say, "Hello TWAT." There have been complaints.
Thanks x

Hi all,
From next week we will be restarting our Student Of The Week Award. Winning pupils will receive a certificate, a badge and a huge bar of chocolate, which 9Z will steal off them at break just before flushing their head down the toilet.
Thanks x

Hi all,
Last week's Learning Walks have shown us that, even though some of your lessons were good, not all of you had The Academy logo, the learning objectives, and 3 differentiated tasks to take into account our VAK learners, on every slide of your PowerPoint. Fix it!
Thanks x

Hi all,
We have put out a list of which colour each subject's exercise books should be for the next academic year. Please make sure that you order the correct colour. If you are unable to find your subject on the list, you should probably start looking for another job.
Thanks x

Hi all,
Thanks to all who brought in Easter Eggs for the charity raffle (ferret rescue). Sadly, Mrs Neighbour decided to store them in the boiler room. This morning she arrived to a chocolate river akin to that in Wonka's factory. If you could bring in some more, we'd love it.
Thanks x

Hi all,
The guest speaker for tonight's 4 hour CPD has, unfortunately, had to cancel. So we've decided that our Head of Teaching and Learning will deliver the session instead. She's had a look at his website and got some screen grabs, so it'll probably be just the same.
Thanks x

Hi all,
We have had contractors in The Academy this weekend, making the car park spaces smaller. This will ensure that everyone will get a parking space but also that anyone arriving after 7:30am may have to get out of their car through the sunroof or rear window.
Thanks x

Hi all,
Mrs Thompson in Art has asked me to point out that all of the posters advertising her new KS Art Club have been vandalised. Sadly, more pupils turned up to her Fart Club than have ever attended her Art Club. They're going to need a bigger room with better ventilation.
Thanks x

Hi all,
Instead of recruiting staff to future vacancies at The Academy, we have decided to put them out to tender. Just send a CV to HR (Carole) with your minimum salary expectation and a list of subjects you could probably teach. You'll be happy and we'll save money.
Thanks x

Hi all,
The Saint Patrick's Day event in The Academy canteen was a huge success. The green burgers, on green buns, and green potatoes with green cheese and green mayonnaise. Weirdly, when I congratulated the kitchen staff they had no idea what I was talking about.
Thanks x

Hi all,
There have been several complaints from parents and in the local media about our RSE curriculum. I can assure you all that we are doing nothing "untoward" in any RSE lessons and the folder marked "Oral Exams" was supposed to have gone into the MFL folder.
Thanks x

Hi all,
Our social media accounts have been hacked again. Please inform your tutor groups that Frazzles the Academy Therapy Dog is alive and well, and we are definitely NOT auditioning for a new dog using Britain's Got Talent criteria on Monday or at any time.
Thanks x

Hi all,
Don't forget that on Saturday morning The Academy is hosting the regional under 15s football semi-final between The Willows and St Hilda's Institute of Technology. Let's hope that TWAT comes out on top of SHIT again. It's in the calendar as directed time.
Thanks x

Hi all,
There has been a mix up on the VLE: tomorrow's lesson "Shiny, Textured, or Smooth?" should have been posted in the GCSE Resistant Materials folder, and not the Year 10 Sex Ed folder. Apologies for any confusion.
Thanks x

Hi all,
Please congratulate Colin Clarkson from Computing. He has successfully completed his NPQSL and has been awarded a pair of scuffed brown brogues, with one shoe lace much longer than the other, to wear around The Academy.
Thanks x

Hi all,
As it's Lesson Observations next week, we thought we'd let you know that the new criteria for "Excellent" are listed in a 500 page document on the Google drive. We expect to see evidence of all 1500 of them in the ten minutes or so we'll be in your classroom.
Thanks x

Hi all,
Tonight's CPD is all about Teaching and Assessment. I recently overheard our CEO and Principal lamenting the lack of any decent T and A in The Academy since the Head of French left, so now things are about to change.
Thanks x

Hi all,
Just a reminder that no cars over 5 years old are permitted on Academy premises. Cars with a 67 plate must now be parked off site, at least four streets away, or they'll be crushed. Tina, you're not fooling anyone with that private plate you got for your 40th.
Thanks x

Hi all,
There is another error in this week's staff newsletter: 9Z's new pupils are the "Farrell twins", not the "feral twins". So far their managed move is going well.
Thanks x

Hi all,
When the site staff were clearing out the old shipping containers to create a new Dance Studio, they discovered 3 pallets of blue highlighters. From today you are to highlight all students' mistakes in blue highlighter whilst adhering to the current mark scheme.
Thanks x

Hi all,
The Academy Trust is trying to save money and has created a new executive role, Business Leader for Overseeing Wastage. If you know anyone who'd be interested in the BLOW job, there are applications on the website or they can see Janice in the back office. Thanks x

Hi all,
We have had to let the new Head of PE go. It turns out he has some GCSEs, doesn't scream at the pupils, he hasn't hit anyone, was seen reading a book, and the final straw, when he arrived at The Academy on Friday, he wasn't wearing shorts. Just not good enough.
Thanks x

Hi all,
Some of you have raised concerns about our most recent Awards Assembly. You're most unhappy with "100% Attendance", "Best Dressed", "Smartest Trainers" and "Nicest Hair and Teeth". Lighten up, we only awarded them to staff.
Thanks x

Hi all,

Our Adult Numeracy and Literacy Evening Classes have been oversubscribed yet again this month. Who would have guessed that "ANAL at TWAT" would have been such a crowd-puller on a cold, wet, Thursday evening.

Thanks x

Hi all,

You may have noticed that your jobs have been advertised on the TES. We are not necessarily getting rid of you but just testing the water to see if we can get much cheaper staff who are just as good as you. We'll "restructure" your roles and make you redundant.

Thanks x

Hi all,

Congratulations to our Teaching and Learning Lead, Mr Johnson. He has finished his NPQ Assessment Research in Secondary Education. The certificate arrived today and we're having a special briefing at 4 o'clock where you can all see him get his ARSE handed to him.

Thanks x

Hi all,

Please do not allow any more pupils to dry their wet things on The Academy's classroom radiators. The whole building stank of wet dogs and cats' pee yesterday and this time it wasn't old Mr Johnson from Science.

Thanks x

Hi all,
Thanks to 9Z for their International Women's Day assembly about Marie Curie. I never knew she had done so much: she discovered radium and polonium, won 2 Nobel prizes and had a worldwide hit with All I Want For Christmas Is You.
Thanks x

Hi all,
The kettle in the staff room is for emergencies only (like the time when my Gaggia was on the blink) and must not be removed under any circumstances. Please do not use it willy-nilly for filling hot water bottles or unfreezing classroom door locks.
Thanks x

Hi all,
The financial year ends soon, please make sure that you spend all your capitation before Easter. Orders must be completed in triplicate (and online using Forms and surveymonkey) and take 28 days to process. Any unspent funds will be taken off next year's budget. Thanks x

Hi all,
Despite us cutting their budget, not replacing their staff, and making them teach in the cold leaky portakabins by the slop bins, the Geography Department still think they are of some use to The Academy. We'll be redeploying them to other subjects from September.
Thanks x

Hi all,

We have another SLT vacancy. This time it's for Coordinator of Curriculum Knowledge. If you can see yourself as The Academy's next COCK, this could be the post for you. Application packs are on the website, Steve.

Thanks x

Hi all,

Just a reminder of the Academy's pen policy:

- Peer marking - vermillion gel pen
- Self marking - cerise gel pen
- Group marking - titian gel pen
- Rough work - smalt
- Neat work - damask
- Teacher marking - bisque week A, cattleya week B
- Tests - 2B pencil
- Exams - jasper

Thanks x

Hi all,

Despite the fact that some subjects do BTEC qualifications and not GCSE exams, we are still going to make all departments set and mark one more mock exam before Easter. This will help us to fairly judge subjects when we are looking at redundancies next term.

Thanks x

Hi all,
Don't forget that as we are now officially in Spring, the heating and hot water in The Academy have been turned off and won't be coming back on until November at the earliest. Make sure you wear extra warm clothes this week, there is snow forecast.
Thanks x

Hi all,
Thanks to all who presented at the Well Being conference on Saturday. We loved Mr Peacock's talk about how he marks 2 sets of books before and after school each day and then Miss Bell told us how she takes every Wednesday off, crying curled up in the foetal position all day.
Thanks x

Hi all,
Next week's Book Scrutiny will focus on the use of your Verbal Feedback Given stamp. We expect to see it used on every page along with a dated and timed comment from you detailing what the feedback was and a signature from the pupil to verify that you did this. Thanks x

Hi all,
Please remember that, unlike some other academies you may have read about, we have agreed that we are not going to measure the length of our students' skirts, make any comments, or force any of them to wear trousers. Unless we can see their balls.
Thanks x

Hi all,
We're putting on some special sessions for anyone aspiring to progress in their career. The Senior Leadership Aspirations Group will meet at 7pm on Fridays, straight after compulsory well-being activities. We hope many of you will want to become Academy SLAGs.
Thanks x

Hi all,
Sad to report that the 9Z Geography Trip to Iceland was an unmitigated disaster: - some pupils and staff turned up late for the bus - Boy Jayden stole two baskets and three trolleys - Colin was discovered in one of the freezers by a security guard at around 9pm.
Thanks x

Hi all,
Today is the start of our 8th set of Year 11 Mock Exams. This morning is English Language and Literature and this afternoon it's Maths. Triple Science is on Monday. Options subjects are on Tuesday. Results are due in sims by 9am on Wednesday. Have a good weekend.
Thanks x

Hi all,
Don't forget today is World Book Day, Year 8 BCG injections, Year 6 Induction Day, Fire Drill Period 3, Core Subject Book Looks, History is being Deep Dived, Year 7 exams, Class Photos, Mocksted, Year 10 Parents' Evening, Staff Briefing (5pm), and SLT interviews.
Thanks x

Hi all,

World Book Day was a huge success. The CEO judged the costumes and prizes went to Chantelle as Anastasia Steele and Boy Jayden as Christian Gray. Tina was given another verbal warning for her outfit. We're still not convinced Debbie Does Dallas was ever a book.

Thanks x

Hi all,

We have calculated that tomorrow's 4 hour twilight CPD may under run by 10 full minutes. If we let you leave early it could mean some of you would not complete your 1265 hours. Therefore could you please bring some planning or marking with you?

Thanks x

Hi all,

We've appointed Ms Jenkins as the new Assistant Assistant Assistant Vice Assistant Principal to the Vice Principal's Assistant. Her lack of experience, refusal to answer any questions directly, and her ability to totter about in 5 inch heels won the panel over.

Thanks x

Hi all,

As Mrs Jenkins is retiring at Easter we have a vacancy for a Staffroom Gossip. Duties include talking about people loudly whilst standing near them, making comments about the paternity of Ms Royle's kids and asking overweight women if they are pregnant. Tlr2b.

Thanks x

Hi all,
After the issues we had last week with student protests about when they can and can't go to the toilet, we have decided that toilets will be patrolled by Academy employees between 8am and 3pm. Teaching Assistants will now be referred to as Toilet Assistants.
Thanks x

Hi all,
Due to an accounting error at Trust Headquarters, we won't be paying you this month. We are hoping to have this rectified by the end of next month. Just think how rich you'll feel when you get paid twice as much in March.
Thanks x

Hi all,
Due to a mix up in venues on Friday, the Drama Club were all given a BCG injection and all Year 8 boys now have parts in the chorus of West Side Story.
Thanks x

Hi all,
There are rumours that we're scrapping TAs in The Academy. This is totally untrue. We are making them all non-qualified teachers and paying them more. So, if you're a qualified teacher on a fixed contract you should probably start looking for a new job elsewhere.
Thanks x

Hi all,
The Year 7 librarians have been editing the works of Roald Dahl by scribbling out and changing words they think may offend. So far we've got Charlie and the Farmers' Market, Charlie and The Lift, Danny the Non-Competitive Town Socialist, and James and Some Fruit.
Thanks x

Hi all,
To improve your "Well-Being" we've come up with another scheme to make you feel good about what you do. For every set of books you mark (to Academy Standards), you'll get a sticker from your line manager. 500 stickers will get you a free coffee in the canteen.
Thanks x

Hi all,
There have been a few complaints about how many hours The Academy asks you to work and some of you think you've already reached the 1265 hour limit. You should read the small print in your contract. There are plenty of non-qualified teachers queuing up to work here.
Thanks x

Hi all,
We are so pleased that there has been a lot of interest in the Primary, Middle, and Secondary Leadership CPD we are organising for this week's twilight. We've noticed a lot of you commenting on our more recent missives with PMSL.
Thanks x

Hi all,
Remember that tomorrow there's a Behaviour: Detentions and Sanctions Meeting after school. The last BDSM was very well attended, although many of you seemed very confused, underdressed and over-equipped.
Thanks x

Hi all,
Helena, from the MFL department, informs me that there's, yet another, error in the Pupil Newsletter this week. Their latest Eurovision-themed competition is called "A Song for Europe", not "A Snog for Europe". Her therapist has asked that you don't send them any more videos.
Thanks x

Hi all,
Our overseas expansion is going well and we soon hope to welcome Willows Academy North Korea and Shanghai Huangpu Academy Trusts to our MAT. We hope that TWAT's links with WANK and SHAT will be beneficial to all.
Thanks x

Hi all,
Last week's Year 8 Student of the Week Award was a very close call. Simon, in 8C, got the highest mark in the exam and in all this term's assessments, but Ellie wins because she has neater handwriting, is popular and lives in one of the big houses by the park.
Thanks x

Hi all,

Our new mission statement is: Achievement, Responsibility, Success, Excellence. There will be ARSE posters in all classrooms and corridors, on the big screen, a banner outside the main gate and a feature in the local press.

Thanks x

Hi all,

We have discovered that the non-qualified teachers we employ are no worse than the qualified ones. Therefore, from now on, we will only employ non-qualified, gullible youngsters who will do whatever we ask. Mostly school leavers, I imagine.

Thanks x

Hi all,

Can you please remember that there is a booking system for taking classes to the library and that you just can't turn up with your class when you haven't bothered to plan a lesson. During Period 1 today 25 classes turned up and 14 of them had no teacher.

Thanks x

Hi all,

Our new IT contractors are based in North Korea. They are available from 12 noon to 4 pm daily (their time) to sort out any issues. There may be some communication issues as they don't speak any English. Perhaps Señora Rey in the MFL department can translate?

Thanks x

Hi all,
Our social media accounts have been hacked again. Monday is definitely not "Kick a Ginger Day" and we will certainly not be celebrating. It is disgusting, discriminatory, unkind and pathetic. It's also not until the 20th of November.
Thanks x

Hi all,
If you are teaching intervention or revision lessons in the Academy this week, please remember to wrap up warm. To save money we have turned off the heating, electricity and water. There are portable generators available. Bring your own petrol.
Thanks x

Hi all,
We are re-advertising the post of Teacher with Responsibility for Diversity. We had a lot of applications, but mainly from people who thought they would be managing a successful street dance troupe.
Thanks x

Hi all,
We have new IT providers who have informed us that they need to upgrade all our servers immediately. This means that you won't be able to access your account from Monday, so the deadline for Year 10 reports is now Sunday. Have a restful and relaxing weekend.
Thanks x

Hi all,

Thank you for all your hard work this half term. You all deserve a break and should find some time to relax with family and loved ones. Unless you teach Year 11. We'll see you on Monday for five days of intervention and revision lessons.

Thanks x

Hi all,

Today is No Uniform Day. Tutors please collect the money from your groups and send anyone who doesn't have a fiver to the Remove Unit for the day. Please also remember the "if it wobbles, we don't want to see it" rule, Tina.

Thanks x

Hi all,

The PTA is holding its Annual Book Burning event tomorrow evening. Any subversive literature, books about dinosaurs, Take A Break magazines or copies of The Guardian can be left at The Main Reception.

Thanks x

Hi all,

Even though the current Appraisal Cycle doesn't finish until the end of the Academic Year, the closing date for Threshold Applications is Monday. Please bear in mind that, as it is Half Term next week, the final date for submitting your evidence file is tomorrow.

Thanks x

Hi KS4 tutors,

Can you please make your groups aware that they are expected to attend The Academy as normal next week. Remember, that Half Term is only for students who are achieving at least 2 grades above target in all their subjects. Even RE.

Thanks x

Hi all,

Last night's Valentine's disco was a huge success, despite us double booking the hall for our RQT CPD on forming positive relationships with pupils. It gave the teachers the ideal opportunity to practise their role play tasks, though.

Thanks x

Hi all,

Tonight is our fourth Year 11 Parents Evening of the term. Please keep conversations brief. Only comment on the most recent mock exams and, after what happened last year, remember that we don't ever predict grades. Predicted grades are for sims, not parents.

Thanks x

Hi all,

Tomorrow, the local Food Standards Inspectors will be in The Academy taking a look at our canteen facilities. We have given the kitchen staff the day off and hired professional caterers. We're paying them with money from departmental budgets. Obviously.

Thanks x

Hi all,
Just to confirm that tonight's KS3 Valentine's Disco starts at 7pm. Ms Simons and Mr Vickery will be there doing security and using air horns and tasers on any child who starts to get too frisky.
Thanks x

Hi all,
We will no longer be using the mantra "Four legs good, two legs bad" to stop pupils swinging on their chairs. One of our PGCE English trainees has read Animal Farm with 9Z, who are now chanting "Four legs good, two legs better" each time they are reprimanded.
Thanks x

Hi all,
We are going to advertise for a new Teacher of Classics. The last one, Mrs Wolstenholme, knew absolutely nothing about the elements of Greek, Latin, History or Philosophy but just kept playing music by Aretha Franklin, Prince, Duran Duran, Clean Bandit, Kylie, and Aha.
Thanks x

Hi all,
On Friday we caught an RQT giving a pen to a child who was not on the "Disadvantaged register". Please be aware that, here at The Academy, we only help those students who are DA, FSM, SEND or EAL. The member of staff has been sent a letter of Management Advice.
Thanks x

Hi Year 11,

In order to qualify for a Prom Ticket this year, you must satisfy the following criteria:

- 99% minimum attendance
- Mock grades above target
- No negative behaviour points
- Sign a legally binding contract to attend The Willows 6th Form
- Be photogenic Pay £60

Thanks x

Dear parents,

It is with deep sadness that we have been forced to disband The Academy's Army Cadet Force with immediate effect. We honestly thought it was the British Army and can only apologise.

Thanks x

Hi all,

Don't forget your Academy Devices for Monday's 5 hour CPD session: Continuing Use of New Technology and Systems. It's a long title but we just couldn't think of an acronym.

Thanks x

Hi all,

There has been yet another typo in the Student Newsletter. The PE department is organising an Inter-House Darts Championship, and not as published "an Inter-House Farts Championship". Apologies to 9Z who were hoping to win it for Jeremy Clarkson House.

Thanks x

Hi all,
Thank you for your responses to the Work/Life Balance Questionnaire. Almost everyone strongly agreed that CPD should not be on a school day until 7pm so we have decided to move all future CPD sessions to Sunday mornings at 8am. It's what you asked for.
Thanks x

Hi all,
We have a new starter in Year 8 tomorrow. He is a very nice young man but speaks very little English and understands very little. Please be patient with him as he is a long way from home and is really missing Sunderland.
Thanks x

Hi all,
Please refer to the section in the staff handbook entitled "Socialising" (Pages 1326 to 1582. Chapter 512, lines 14-15.) "Staff must not, under any circumstances, socialise with any colleagues who are Senior to them in rank. Not even accidentally. Capeesh?"
Thanks x

Hi all,
Please make sure that you are wearing your TWAT ID badge at all times when on the premises. Mr Gooding forgot his badge yesterday and 9Z spent the whole day following him around shouting "Stranger Danger!" He has worked here for thirty years.
Thanks x

Hi all,
For tomorrow's Book Check Can we please have all pupil books from each group. That's the ones you use in class and the ones we show to Ofsted.
Thanks x

Hi all,
We have a new Year 11 student starting tomorrow. This is not a Managed Move, he's a genuine move. Unfortunately, his previous school has lost all of his coursework, so you'll need to do that all again with him. Also, he needs to complete all the mocks we've done.
Thanks x

Hi all,
Tonight's four hour CPD is all about our new marking policy. You'll need to bring 29 exercise books from each class you teach, 25 different coloured highlighters, 17 biros, your 42 different feedback stampers, a glue stick, coloured paper and some Post Its.
Thanks x

Hi all,
Please spend an hour or two filling in the latest Work/Life Balance Questionnaire. We've cut it down to just 300 questions this time and some of them are multiple choice. You have until 6am tomorrow.
Thanks x

Hi all,

On Wednesday after school we have a careers advisor coming into The Academy to give a presentation about future careers and training opportunities. This isn't for the pupils and we expect all staff without TLRs and all teachers of "arty farty" subjects to attend. Thanks x

Hi all,

Congratulations to Mr Cass who has just completed his NPQSLT in sarcasm. He will be putting on some bespoke training for our RQTs on Wednesday. When I asked if it was going to be in the Main Hall, he replied, "No, outside the kitchen, by the bins." He will go far. Thanks x

Hi all,

Monday is the long awaited, annual 9Z Charity Bake Sale. They have been so busy in the food tech rooms and their fingernails have never been so clean. Cakes cost from £1 but, I believe that if you give them a tenner, they won't force you to eat anything. Thanks x

Hi all,

Just to let you know that we will no longer be using our new speech-to-text software to write the Pupils' Newsletter. Also the Mass Debating Club will go ahead after school on Monday as planned. Thanks x

Hi all,
Just to let you know, the second official round of Appraisal Observations starts on Monday. It coincides with Mock Mock Mocksted, Learning Walks, Peer Observations, Pupil Voice and Book Looks, so some of your classrooms will have more SLT in them than kids.
Thanks x

Hi all,
We have completed this week's book check and quite frankly, we're not impressed. Most books were not up to the required standard, and many of you will be told on Monday that you're on Support Plans and even final warnings. Have a wonderful and relaxing weekend.
Thanks x

Hi all,
Please don't forget that 4pm today is the deadline for entering this week's GCSE mock results into sims. Please include Actual Grades, Target Grades, Aspirational Target Grades and excuses. Covid is no longer a valid excuse. Last week some of you forgot this.
Thanks x

Hi all,
Someone has taken the pencil sharpener from the Geography Department. If any of you know of its whereabouts, please let us know at your earliest convenience. Apparently, they can't teach until it is returned.
Thanks x

Hi all,
We apologise for the events which happened today while staff were picketing the main gates. We had no idea that the sprinklers were timed to go off at 8 minute intervals for the whole day, nor did we realise they were hooked up to the Year 9 boys' toilets. Oops.
Thanks x

Hi all,
We have the results of the staff numeracy tests we gave you on Monday. Mr Giles has worked out that two thirds of you passed and the other 45% will have to retake it this evening.
Thanks x

Hi all,
Please make sure that all of your resources are carefully locked away at all times. The recent thefts in The Academy seem to have been perpetrated by "agents" acting on behalf of the Art department, who have misunderstood the term "reclaimed materials".
Thanks x

Hi all,
We are going to hire a security firm to supervise the lunch queues in The Academy. There's far too much pushing, shouting, queue jumping, bad language, name calling and even violence. And it's almost as bad when the PE staff have gone and the kids turn up.
Thanks x

Hi all,

The poor literacy levels at The Academy are really quite embarrassing. From today, there's a new literacy scheme which certain individuals will attend to help with their basic reading skills. So, it looks like you're going to be covering PE or Geography lessons.

Thanks x

Hi all,

Student Voice tells us homework isn't being done because it's boring and can take up to 15 minutes. Therefore, from Monday, homework tasks must not take more than a minute and must be fun. Teachers will be rated on the quality of tasks by pupils for Appraisal.

Thanks x

Hi all,

Tina's Environmental Carbon Neutral Club is recruiting new members. Please remind your tutors that all the information they need can be found on 1000 laminated A3 flyers posted all over The Academy.

Thanks x

Hi all,

After Kai in Year 10 scored all three goals in the County Cup Semi Final win this morning, he is now on the Gifted and Talented Register. His GCSE targets will change from 3 to 8 in all subjects. Please adjust your seating plans and mark books to reflect this.

Thanks x

Hi all,
The price of coffee and tea in the staffroom drinks machine will be going up from £1 to £3.50 a cup from Monday. Hot chocolate will be £4. Something to do with Brexit, or Ukraine, or the Energy Crisis, or something. Not greed. No.
Thanks x

Hi all,
Don't forget that there are classes tomorrow morning. This is for teachers who are striking next week. In order that students don't miss out on their education to your woke, bolshy, selfish, communist views, you're required to teach Wednesday's lessons tomorrow.
Thanks x

Dear parents,
We will no longer tolerate fast food deliveries by drone. Yesterday, one of our Assistant Vice Principals to an Assistant Vice Principal received 3rd degree burns from a badly flown KFC gravy bucket. She's OK but her walkie-talkie and hi viz jacket are ruined.
Thanks x

Hi all,
The counsellor has asked me to inform you that Chantelle is having a rough time at the moment and might not be as cooperative, pleasant, or attentive as usual. Apparently, her trainers are only the second most expensive ones available and her life is now over.
Thanks x

Hi all,
Four weeks into the 2nd term seems like a good time to have a crackdown on uniform. Tutors check that all students are in full uniform, no make-up, no jewellery and school approved footwear. Tutors phone parents with any problems and leadership won't support you.
Thanks x

Hi all,
The most recent Pupil Voice says that behaviour is getting worse and there is no incentive to complete work or attend lessons. So, starting tomorrow we are scrapping negative behaviour points and giving Mars Bars to anyone who turns up and completes anything.
Thanks x

Hi all,
Can we please make sure that our PGCE trainees are supervised at all times? When the History one was being gaffer-taped to a chair and hoisted up to the ceiling by 9Z, Tina was at big McDonalds getting Chantelle a Big Mac as a reward for bringing a pen.
Thanks x

Hi all,
The latest progress data drop is due tomorrow. Please enter the correct letter into sims for each student: B - Below, U - Up to scratch, or M - Mastering. We expect all students to be aware of their own personal BUM grades, should they be asked by Ofsted or SLT.
Thanks x

Hi all,

Looking at the latest GCSE mock data we can see that Mrs Searle has done wonders with 11D with all of them getting 2 grades above target. She is now going to swap groups with me and take 11A who are all 3 grades below target. Her Appraisal is now based on this.

Thanks x

Hi all,

After the students' four letter word protest about the quality of our school meals today, the canteen will no longer be serving Alphabetti Spaghetti or Alphabites.

Thanks x

Hi all,

We have some building work starting today. This is not the long promised new library block or extra classrooms to help with the overcrowding but a new centre for SLT to work and have meetings. There's so many of us now that the board room isn't big enough.

Thanks x

Hi all,

Someone has hacked the VLE and uploaded some disgusting material. Doctored photos of SLT, pornography, and worst of all, Overtime Claim Forms. The ICT department, Tom, is deleting them as we speak.

Thanks x

Hi all,

Mr Jenkins will not be returning to The Academy. We have shared out his timetable with anyone who has too many frees on their timetable and with the people who waste their lunchtimes in the staffroom, eating lunch and chatting.

Thanks x

Hi all,

To fix the problem of the leaking roof in the main building, our Head of Premises, Mr Stephen Barclay, has blown the whole budget on buckets to catch the water.

Thanks x

Hi all,

There has been another error in this week's Academy Newsletter. The sentence about Open Evening should say: "Mme Lefevre will offer visitors the opportunity to sample the delights of her tasty French cuisine" not "her tasty French cousin." We can only apologise.

Thanks x

Hi all,

Some of you have been wearing the wrong hi-viz on break duty, so here's a reminder: SLT get a fleece-lined waterproof hi-viz jacket with built in Wi-Fi and heat pad and the rest of you get a Pound Shop hi-viz gilet that will tear as soon as you look at it.

Thanks x

Hi all,

Thanks to those who completed The Academy's most recent 500 hundred question Anonymous Well-Being Questionnaire. I still don't have responses from Steve, Tina, Gary and Sue. Also, 19 of you need to make appointments to speak to HR during your next free lesson.

Thanks x

Hi all,

We have been informed that, for GDPR reasons, we are no longer allowed to put pupils' names on exercise books. From Monday, pupil books will be identified by stains or smells.

Thanks x

Hi all,

Due to an error in the TES advert we placed for a Teacher of Physics, we will now be interviewing for a Teacher of Psychics. Nobody could have foreseen that.

Thanks x

Hi all,

We feel we must apologise to all our vegan teachers and pupils after we caught kitchen staff tippexing out the letter G on cartons of Goat Milk, after last week's Oat Milk order failed to arrive. None of you noticed and they're blaming Brexit, so no harm done.

Thanks x

Hi all,

Please read the "Unions" section of the Staff Handbook and be aware that, if you strike next month, not only are you ruining the children's education, but you will never be promoted, have a top set, pass your Appraisal, or have an indoor break duty ever again.

Thanks x

Hi all,

Due to the cold weather we are relaxing the uniform rules. For this week only students may wear an Academy branded hoodie in lessons. No other hoodies are permitted. Academy hoodies can be bought from our website from £32.99 and usually take 4 weeks to arrive.

Thanks x

Hi all,

Just to let you know that the school nurse no longer works for the NHS but a private contractor (Willows Medical Ltd). Pupils will still be allowed to make appointments with her but their parents will be invoiced £160 a time. Plus VAT. Obvs.

Thanks x

Hi all,

We have quite a lot of staff off sick at the moment and really appreciate everyone going above and beyond, rallying around, and doing quite a lot of cover. Also, don't forget the Mini-Mocksted, Learning Walks and Book Analyses are this week.

Thanks x

Hi all,
Sadly, the ovens in the canteen have been condemned by those health and safety jobsworths. Therefore we are asking all staff if they could please bring in a microwave, a kettle, a camping stove, hair straighteners or a Breville sandwich maker to help us out.
Thanks x

Hi all,
The Geography Department's move from the second floor to the ground floor has been postponed. Apparently, they need to do a traffic survey first and then colour a land use map, before taking samples of water from the condensation puddles on the window sills.
Thanks x

Hi all,
I just noticed another spelling error in the staff bulletin. It should say, "Pay your milk club subs to Tina." not "Pay your milf club subs to Tina." At least, I hope it's an error.
Thanks x

Hi all,
Just to let you know that we have moved Wednesday's book check to Monday. Please be in The Academy at 7:30am, standing at your designated trestle table in the hall, with all of your books marked up to date. We will probably look at three of them.
Thanks x

Hi all,
Sadly, there was yet another error in this week's Academy Newsletter. It should read, "The whole of Year 10 will be off timetable on Wednesday" not "The whore of Year 10 will be off timetable on Wednesday".
Thanks x

Hi all,
There was a major safeguarding incident yesterday when Tina told Janice she loved her outfit and that not many people could pull it off. Chantelle accepted the challenge.
Thanks x

Hi all,
Tonight's material for the CPD session "Cognitive Review for Assessing Progress" is on the VLE. Please make sure you have familiarised yourself with all the CRAP documents beforehand.
Thanks x

Hi all,
It seems that some of you are not differentiating your lessons for our disadvantaged students. Therefore we have decided that you will now write a separate lesson plan for every child for every lesson you teach.
Thanks x

Hi all,
We've a vacancy for a Caretaker. The job involves:
- walking around carrying stepladders for no reason
- putting desks and chairs out facing the wrong way during exam week
- hiding in the office, smoking
- switching off all the lights during Parents' Evening
Thanks x

Hi all,
Please remember that, as The Academy's new exorcist doesn't start work until Monday, no Key Stage 3 pupils must be allowed to go to the first floor toilets by themselves.
Thanks x

Hi all,
Just a reminder that when teaching Sex Ed you must use the official Academy videos on the VLE and not the clip of Mr Johnson and Tina in the Arndale Centre after the Christmas Night Out that Janice downloaded from the Crimestoppers website.
Thanks x

Hi all,
Please do not mention Chantelle's hair. We've spoken to the Head of Science and she's agreed that a can of hairspray, Marlboro Lights, a box of matches and a Van de Graaff Generator are probably not the best things to leave out when 9Z are coming into class.
Thanks x

Hi all,
Due to a misunderstanding by our new canteen manager, today's Vegan Special will no longer be Toad in The Hole. Just Toad. Sorry for any inconvenience.
Thanks x

Hi all,
We have a new Duty Team rota starting tomorrow. If you are an ECT, PGCE Trainee, or had a negative GCSE residual last summer, you'll be outside, especially if it's raining. Bring a coat.
Thanks x

Hi all,
Don't forget that Wednesday is the Year 9 Options Evening. Please be aware that it is not a competition between departments. However, if you don't get at least 60 "definites", we will be scrapping your subject.
Thanks x

Hi all,
We will shortly be advertising for another Head of Geography. We thought we had finally found someone last week, her track record is legendary but it turns out that all of her worksheets had been pre-coloured in.
Thanks x

Hi all,

From tomorrow Year 11 are starting their new 15 period day. Lesson 1 starts at 5:30am and lesson 15 will finish at 8pm. We will be giving the students a full hour for lunch. Staff can consider this PPA time. Homework will be set, marked and feedback given daily.

Thanks x

Hi all,

Our new Assistant Head in Charge of Behaviour Policy has asked that you stop sending children to him if they are misbehaving or not following our high expectations. He is only in charge of the behaviour policy, not the practical side.

Thanks x

Hi all,

Please remember that, after several hundred parental complaints, we are no longer using the Written Teacher Feedback stamps and have replaced them with the new Feeding Forward Strategies stamp. Please collect one from the office on Monday.

Thanks x

Hi all,

At some point over the next few days we'll be having a fire drill. Year 11 will not have to go outside for any fire alarms. If you teach Year 11 just carry on teaching. Our GCSE results are much more important than the lives of a few kids or staff.

Thanks x

Hi all,
I'd like to thank our new Assistant Head with Responsibility for Positive Mindset, Mr Sunak, for his amazing talk to the Year 11s yesterday. Although, instead of repeating the word "mindset" over and over, he probably could have mentioned "hard work", too.
Thanks x

Hi all,
Don't forget that Level One of our new 25 step Behaviour Policy is no longer the reprimand, but the eye roll. Please remember that eyes should be rolled from left to right and that there should be no tutting until Level 2. We've already had parental complaints.
Thanks x

Hi all,
Tutors, please remember to complete the following during the 10 minutes you have with your class today: register and lunches, check uniform and shoes, check makeup and hairstyles, check equipment, show PowerPoint, read The Academy Prayer, give out timetables.
Thanks x

Hi all,
Today's 25 15 minute CPD sessions will seem like a lot to take in, especially for our newest colleagues, but please remember that you have until Monday to have evidence of all of them in your lessons. Learning Walks start then.
Thanks x

Hi all,
Welcome back to The Academy. This morning's 1st CPD session is entitled "Get down with the kids: creating relationships and being more street". You'll be taken on a tour of slang, gestures and teeth kissing from a man in his 50s who often forgets what day it is.
Thanks x

Hi all,
Now that the local river has almost thawed, the PE department is going to restart its Canoeing, Rowing, and Punting Club. Sign up on the staff room notice board. The first 10 members get a TWAT CRAP Club hoodie.
Thanks x

Hi all,
Many of you have contacted The Academy to ask whether we are returning to work today or tomorrow. I can confirm that this information is on the VLE.
Thanks x

Dear parents,
We feel that the posters for The Academy Robotics Club may have been a little misleading and we are aware of your concerns. "Join Robotics Club and make new friends" meant other students, not creating new friends. Please don't worry.
Thanks x

Hi all,
Unfortunately, we have had to postpone our Awards Evening on Wednesday. Our guest speaker, and most successful student ever, has had to cancel because they won't let him change his shifts at Wetherspoons. The twilight CPD will go ahead as planned.
Thanks x

Hi all,
Our new Assistant Vice Assistant to the Assistant Vice Principal's Assistant Head of Unnecessary Paperwork has created a new format for Schemes of Learning and Lesson Plans. They are to be completed in triplicate from next week. They'll be available on the VLE.
Thanks x

Hi all,
At this time of year, we think about New Year's Resolutions. So, I've written a resolution for all of you which you must keep for 12 months. They are linked to your Appraisal and will affect any future pay rises.
Thanks x

Hi all,
For Tuesday's CPD we'll be doing a different kind of ice breaker task. The boiler burst on Wednesday, flooded the ground floor and all the water froze. It's about 6 inches thick. You'll need to bring hammers, salt, a lot of towels and ice skates.
Thanks x

Hi all,

Just a reminder that your new employment contract starts as of midnight tonight. Anyone who has not signed and returned the new terms and conditions is effectively resigning. We'd also like to wish you all a Happy New Year.

Thanks x

Hi all,

There's been a change to next week's CPD schedule. Instead of a day of icebreakers, we will be doing team building tasks. This means that you'll all be helping English, Maths, Technology, Computing and Music to move to their new rooms, while they put up displays.

Thanks x

Hi all,

The latest book checks show that some students are self marking in damson or plum coloured pen when you know that the only permitted colours are elderberry or fig. Please rectify this next week.

Thanks x

Hi all,

We have decided to revamp the marking policy and to cut down the 150 or so codes we are currently using to 87. We will also be using fewer colours, replacing the current 29 colours to a much more manageable 27.

Thanks x

Hi all,
Just to let you know that from next week, daily staff briefings will be in the main hall at 7:45am. Attendance is compulsory. Then, about an hour later you will receive an email from an Associate Vice Principal contradicting all the information from the briefing.
Thanks x

Hi all,
Unfortunately, due to budget constraints , we will no longer be providing a buffet lunch for all staff on the first day back in January. The money we save will be spent on specialist CPD for SLT; a working lunch at that new 5 star restaurant in the town centre.
Thanks x

Hi all,
For Wednesday's INSET, our new Assistant Vice Principal in charge of arranging 1st day back training has planned a full day of Ice Breaker activities. This will help us get to know the 37 new staff. The Academy will be open until 9pm so you can plan for Thursday.
Thanks x

Hi all,
If you ring in sick, cancelling your planned GCSE Revision or Intervention sessions, it's not a good idea to be interviewed live on ITV News in the Next Sale queue, Tina.
Thanks x

Hi all,

Starting next term, we have paid some highly respected education experts to come into The Academy to provide Ofsted Training. They'll tell us we're doing fine/terribly, sell us their latest book/software, cash the cheque and disappear leaving us none the wiser.

Thanks x

Hi all,

Next week, we have 27 new staff starting at The Academy. 20 are ECTs and 7 SLT. Be nice to them and remember that the SLT will be trying to put their own personal stamp on Academy life and must be shown respect. Some of them have up to three years' experience.

Thanks x

Hi all,

I hope you're enjoying the Christmas break? Thank you to all who met last night's 7pm KS3 data deadline. It's Improvement Plans for the rest of you.

Thanks x

Hi all,

If you take a lot of time off work with chronic back pain, it's probably not a good idea to post a video clip of yourself winning your local pub's Christmas Limbo Competition on Tiktok. You have, literally, reached a new low, Janice.

Thanks x

Hi all,

A Happy Christmas to all Academy Staff! Now, if you've got time to waste on social media, you should probably make a start marking those GCSE mock papers.

Thanks x

Hi all,

Just a reminder that The Academy will be closed tomorrow so all GCSE intervention and revision sessions are to be held on ZOOM. Please make sure that sessions are recorded so students who don't turn up (and your line managers) can watch them later.

Thanks x

Hi all,

We have decided that Deep Diving Departments during term time is time consuming and difficult due to there being kids everywhere. Therefore, we have decided that all future Deep Dives will be done at weekends or during holidays. We'll start with Art next Friday.

Thanks x

Hi all,

This week there has been a team of Associate Assistant Assistant Vice-Assistant Vice Principals in The Academy doing book checks in every subject with a 120 point check list. Your Appraisal is based on this. We'll let you know if you're successful in January.

Thanks x

Hi all,

The Academy Brass Band's performance in the shopping centre last night was amazing. They worked through their repertoire of Carols and hymns and drew a huge crowd, allowing 9Z ample opportunity to work through the pockets and handbags of the unwary shoppers.

Thanks x

Hi all,

Sorry your pay rise wasn't included in this month's salary payment. In the meeting when we were due to discuss this, we spent far too much time arguing which is best, Penguins or Hobnobs. It's Hobnobs, obvs. Penguins are just chocolate covered bourbons.

Thanks x

Hi all,

From January we are using a new scheme to help GCSE students prepare for their futures. The Academic Record of Secondary Education will be a folder containing all of their grades from Year 7 until they leave. They'll be proud to show future employers their ARSE.

Thanks x

Hi all,

We've been looking at next term's calendar and have found a glaring error. There is CPD twilight session calendared for Sunday the 5th of February from 3:30 until 6pm. This is, of course, wrong. It should say "from 3:30 until 7pm".

Thanks x

Hi all,

We have been looking at the scripts we use when reprimanding students and have decided, after several complaints from uncomfortable staff and stupid grins from silly boys, to remove the phrase "I'd like you to think about it long and hard".

Thanks x

Hi all,

Even though it is the holidays, we're still doing Well-Being Wednesday tomorrow. You must take 20 minutes out of your day to do one of the activities in the Approved Academy Well-Being Activities List, film yourself doing it, and upload it to the VLE before 4pm. Thanks x

Hi all,

Last night's Academy Carol Service was a great success. However, there were a couple of errors in the programme: Shepherds Pie Carol should have read Shepherds' Pipe Carol and it should have said O Little Town of Bethlehem, not O Little Clown of Bethlehem.

Thanks x

Hi all,

If you're one of the people who left The Academy on Friday, you'll probably by now have realised that the envelope we gave you was empty. I'm sure your department will have bought you something though, so it's not all bad news.

Thanks x

Hi all,
If you're coming to The Academy today to deliver intervention lessons, please bring a sweater and some gloves. The heating is turned off until 4th of January. Remember, that use of any electrical heating device which has not been PAT tested is a sackable offence. Thanks x

Hi all,
As some classrooms were extremely untidy when you all left, we have hired some contract cleaners to come in over the break. They have orders to throw away everything that isn't safely stored in a cupboard or a drawer. Any personal effects will be binned.
Thanks x

Hi all,
I hope you're enjoying the Christmas Break and managing to de-stress after a hectic term. Sadly, due to a computer virus, all the data from last week's assessments has been corrupted. You must all come into The Academy tomorrow and re-enter all data before 11am.
Thanks x

Hi all,
Last night's Christmas talent show went really well, apart from a couple of incidents. Kylie Johnson in year 7 had a bit of a mishap during her guitar solo when her G string snapped and Chantelle's Dance of the Seven Veils had to be cut short for the same reason.
Thanks x

Hi all,

I've emailed out the new template for lesson plans starting next term. It's only three pages per lesson, you'll soon get used to it. They have to be with line managers a week in advance so you have until the 27th, which is almost 2 weeks. Happy Christmas.

Thanks x

Hi all,

There has been another error in this week's Pupil Newsletter. Sadie Porritt in 11H has not won a prize for her "outstanding ginger beard" but her "outstanding gingerbread". We can only apologise.

Thanks x

Hi all,

Here's the agenda for this afternoon's Briefing:

- 3:30 prompt start
- 3:45 PE department arrive after having gone that extra mile
- 4:00 SLT introduce new Rewards and Behaviour policies for January
- 6:00 Leavers' speeches (there's just 30 leaving this term)
- 9:00 End

Thanks x

Dear parents,
We are pleased to see that, during the inclement weather, our students have been wearing sensible footwear to The Academy. However, many of them seem to be wearing supermarket wellies. Only branded, official TWAT wellington boots (£28.99) are permitted.
Thanks x

Hi all,
Please remember that you are entirely responsible for your parking space in the car park. You should keep it free from ice and snow and are responsible for gritting it in the winter. Keeping your parking space pristine is now part of The Academy's Appraisal Process.
Thanks x

Hi all,
There was another error in this week's Staff Newsletter. The PE Department will not be having "exercise bonks" next year as reported, but "exercise books".
Thanks x

Hi all,
Thanks to everyone who helped out at the Senior Citizens Christmas Party yesterday. There was just the one incident when Boy Jayden's great grandfather fell out of his wheelchair during the hokey cokey, we discovered he was sitting on 5 brand new staff laptops.
Thanks x

Hi all,

Ladies, please refer to the "Heel Height to Salary equation" in the staff handbook for clarification about your footwear. Heels are only for those with a TLR3+ and 4 inch heels are a privilege for only the most important of us. ECTs should be wearing flats.

Thanks x

Hi all,

Please remember to fill in this term's Staff Well Being Questionnaire before you leave this evening after our 4 hour Pushing The iPad Trolley Safely CPD. Be as honest as you can; it is completely anonymous. Email it to me from your Academy email before 9pm.

Thanks x

Hi all,

For tomorrow's Christmas Jumper Day can we please make sure that we are not wearing any suggestive or obscene pullovers? Nobody has ever wanted to squeeze your baubles, Janice.

Thanks x

Hi all,

On Friday, one of our new trainee teachers reported that Chantelle had called him a "See You Next Tuesday". We have assured him that we are taking this matter very seriously and will deal with it as soon as we figure out what a "SYNT" is.

Thanks x

Hi all,
We are incredibly pleased that 9Z decided to open and run their own soup kitchen to help those less fortunate in our local community. We are less pleased that they wanted to call it "The Brothel".
Thanks x

Hi all,
We feel we must apologise for the quality of last Friday's Academy Christmas Lunch. To say it was inedible was an understatement. However, it's not all bad news, as the Site Team have been using the leftover stuffing to fill the potholes in the staff car park.
Thanks x

Hi all,
I can't apologise enough for the stress caused by 9Z during yesterday's assembly. When the Head of Year 9, Mr Gough, agreed to let them do an assembly, he thought it was going to be about "Seaworld" not "the C word".
Thanks x

Hi all,
Just a reminder that if a child should give you a Christmas present, you must declare it to HR via the Google form. All gifts will be raffled during our final briefing, unless it is alcohol, which is banned on the premises and must be given to me straight away.
Thanks x

Hi all,

Just a week to go and a quick reminder that here at The Academy we teach right up to the final bell on the 22nd of December. Any member of staff deviating from their official, approved Schemes of Learning will face disciplinary action. Have a good weekend.

Thanks x

Hi all,

Today is a busy day in The Academy. Our local primary feeders will be attending our musical nativity at 10am, it's the old folks' Christmas party at lunchtime, the KS3 disco at 12:30pm, the Talent Show all afternoon and Appraisal observations all day.

Thanks x

Hi all,

Tonight is the Christmas Concert at the local Retirement Village. The Academy Choir will be performing and everyone is welcome. Mrs Henderson will be there from 6:30 to go through some Christmas music and 9Z will be there from 6:00 to go through some handbags.

Thanks x

Hi all,

As there are two weeks until the end of term, we have ample time to do another round of GCSE Mock Exams for Year 11 and Year 10. They must have completed all of the past exams papers available by now, so you have until Monday to write and print some new ones.

Thanks x

Hi all,

During Friday's Christmas lunch we're doing a twist on a festive tradition. Instead of searching for a thrupenny bit in the Christmas Pudding, this year one lucky person will find Mrs Brown's glass eye. She got a little carried away during the mixing process.

Thanks x

Hi all,

There's just two weeks left before we break up for the Christmas break, or as we now call it Festive Revisiontide. The Academy will be open every day, except Christmas Day for GCSE revision sessions. We are doing Zoom lessons only on the 25th. We're not monsters.

Thanks x

Hi all,

Would whoever it is who is printing those 30000 Christmas word searches on the staff room photocopier please at least have the decency to keep refilling the paper tray and keep an eye out for paper jams.

Thanks x

Hi all,

Just a polite reminder that if you are not well enough to attend The Academy then you're probably not well enough to be interviewed on the local TV news whilst Christmas shopping in the Arndale Centre, Diannah.

Thanks x

Hi all,

It's not too late to put your name down for Next Friday's Academy Christmas Lunch. For just £22.50 + VAT you can enjoy a chlorinated turkey slice, stuffing, roast potatoes, some kind of green vegetable things and either Christmas pudding or (alcohol free) trifle.

Thanks x

Hi all,

We'd like to thank the Music Department after the Christmas Performances of Mary Poppins were a total sell out. This was due, in part, to Tina's "wardrobe malfunction" on the opening night after which the Technology Department put up "Mary Popsout" posters.

Thanks x

Hi all,

After the Local Health Inspectors visited The Academy canteen last week, and produced a damning report, we've been forced to publish an apology. So here it is: "There is no nutritional value in sawdust and we are truly sorry that we were found out. Obvs."

Thanks x

Hi all,

This week, because we care about the welfare of all our stakeholders, we are reintroducing SEAL. KS3 classes will be working on social skills, KS4 and staff will be looking at friendships and empathy, and 9Z will be balancing beach balls on their noses.

Thanks x

Hi all,

We have too many Associate Assistant's Associate Assistant Headteachers. Rather than sackings, we've decided to have a competition. I'm An SLT Get Me Out Of Here will run next week. Staff will have to do inappropriate "trials"and pupils will get to vote them out.

Thanks x

Hi all,

There was an error in this week's pupils' newsletter. The lunchtime Christmas entertainment events section should read "brass band" and not "bras banned". Sorry if you've had nightmares.

Thanks x

Hi all,

Due to the fact that they are a fire hazard (and we let our insurance lapse to save a few pounds), we have banned all Christmas trees and decorations in the Academy. We will be showing a fully decorated Christmas tree on the big screen at breaks and at lunch.

Thanks x

Hi all,

Last night's Christmas Talent Show was a huge success. Sadly, we didn't get to see Janice and Tina's Cheeky Girls Tribute Act as they were picked up near the bus stop by the local vice squad and charged with soliciting.

Thanks x

Hi all,

If you have an Advent Calendar in your classroom, please make sure that it is locked away when the room is unoccupied. We just spotted Tina on the CCTV, running around The Academy with a carrier bag full of tiny chocolates.

Thanks x

Hi all,

We are having an imposed joint twilight CPD session next Monday which will be led by colleagues from our sister Academy, Saint Hilda's Institute of Technology. I have no doubt there'll be surprising results when SHIT and TWAT get together.

Thanks x

Hi all,

Carole in the office has won a Caribbean Cruise and will not be in The Academy for 2 weeks. This means, from Monday, reception will be manned by Chantelle and Boy Jayden as part of their work experience. Please do not invite any guests on site until January.

Thanks x

Hi all,

Sad to report that Mr Jameson has left The Academy. Shortly after asking "Do Ofsted really want to see this? Or are you just telling us this so we'll do it without question?" in last night's CPD, there was a surprise drugs raid by the police and he was arrested.

Thanks x

Hi all,
Tomorrow you will be given a new fob to sign in and out of The Academy. At the end of each week this new system will allow us to publish a list of who the hardest working teachers are, i.e. those who are here the longest, and also who the skivers are.
Thanks x

Hi all,
As we're very concerned about our standing in the local community and need to be on our best behaviour at all times, our CEO has decreed that everyone going on the Staff Christmas Night Out on Saturday will be required to wear their Academy Hi Viz at all times.
Thanks x

Hi all,
We need to be doing more for our Disadvantaged Students to "level up" and "bridge the gap". Therefore, we have decided that every DS will get their own Personal Assistant from within their class, who will be responsible for organising their life and equipment.
Thanks x

Hi all,
We have a vacancy for a SENCO, or whatever they're called these days. We've no idea what the job entails, we think it's mainly giving coloured paper to specky kids and looking after the social rejects (pupils not staff). It's non-teaching so pays £17K per annum.
Thanks x

Hi all,
Don't forget that, as a part of our community outreach, we are still collecting for the local food bank. To try to involve students and staff more, there is a prize for the oldest can of food. Last year's record was a can of Finefare rhubarb with a sell by date from 1982.
Thanks x

Hi all,
After Mr Jones "left The Academy by mutual consent" on Friday, we're looking for a PE teacher. If you know anyone who makes sexist jokes, wears shorts and sliders all year round, shouts a lot but only uses words of one syllable and is illiterate, they'd be ideal.
Thanks x

Hi all,
Due to us "settling out of court with a former employee", we have decided that having a tattoo is no longer a sackable offence.
However, if you have one we don't like, you will be sent to Chantelle's Uncle Spider to have it turned into The Academy's coat of arms.
Thanks x

Hi all,
Starting on Monday, any child not in full uniform, including school shoes, blazer, tie, Academy Coat and an Academy Backpack, will be sent home. Obviously, this doesn't include anyone from 9Z, or any PP, FSM, LAC or SEND kids... but definitely all the others.
Thanks x

Hi all,

Be aware that Chantelle has had her other eyebrow pierced and is wearing a three inch bolt through it, which is pulling her face down. Please don't comment on it. She's just attention seeking. She has not had a stroke.

Thanks x

Hi all,

We have a lunchtime supervisor vacancy. We have 3 nice ones, so we're looking for the kind of person who ignores the crying softies, has a crafty fag behind the gym, will give a child with a broken leg a wet paper towel, and will happily slap kids if they act up.

Thanks x

Hi all,

To try to cut down on internal truancies we have fitted timer locks to all classroom doors. They will lock 5 minutes after the bell and open a minute before the end of lessons. We will be releasing a pack of rabid dogs, or 9Z, during lesson times.

Thanks x

Hi all,

We just noticed another error in this week's staff bulletin. The Deep Dive of the Geography Department is not next Thursday, it's today. Sorry. I hope you're all ready?

Thanks x

Hi all,

Yesterday's Book Looks went OK, although some students' books still don't have detailed teacher marking and pupil feedback for every activity in every lesson this term. Please make sure that this is rectified before the next round of "Drop Ins" starts on Monday.

Thanks x

Hi all,

I just wanted to thank you all for attending last night's 5 hour CPD, "How to manage your time effectively." Please make sure that you complete all 300 questions in the attached feedback questionnaire before 5pm today.

Thanks x

Hi all,

For tomorrow's Well-Being Wednesday we are having a special Christmas Crafts CPD. Please bring felt tip pens, glue, glitter and card and you'll be making Christmas cards and Advent Calendars until 7pm. Also, just a reminder that Book Checks begin on Thursday.

Thanks x

Hi all,

Due to the current wet weather, all duty personnel will be assigned a classroom and a class to look after during break and lunch. Pupils are supposed to read quietly but will mostly throw things around, use their phones and draw penises on the steamed up windows.

Thanks x

Hi all,

Congratulations to Tom who has won the regional Teacher Of The Year Award. However, we have taken the trophy off him and are giving it to Janet who we consider to be a much better teacher. She will be presented with it by our CEO at the next Awards Evening.

Thanks x

Hi all,

We have made a list of all the pupils who didn't pay their pound for our Children In Need non uniform day on Friday. Please read it out in registration tomorrow. We will write to parents and deny their offspring access to free school lunches until it is paid.

Thanks x

Hi all,

We have three new TAs starting this week. They won't be helping pupils in lessons, we've employed them to replace the three maths teachers who left at half term. We're going to save a fortune on supply.

Thanks x

Hi all,

You may notice on Monday that each classroom will contain 40 tables and chairs. I would like to reassure you that this is to free up some storage space and definitely not because we're merging some classes. You will also get a new teaching timetable.

Thanks x

Hi all,

We've discovered that 9Z's Children In Need Slushies contained Red Bull, vodka, and the hand sanitiser left over from when we took Covid seriously. The £500 they raised will go straight to the local hospital's children's chronic liver disease and blindness wards.

Thanks x

Hi all,

There has been another error in The Academy Staff Newsletter. The new Year 9 starting on Monday and transferring from the PRU is called Violet Stalker and is not, as previously reported, a "violent stalker". Not as far as we know, anyway.

Thanks x

Hi all,

Today is The Academy's Non Uniform Day. Most of the money will go to Children in Need but I need a new chair, too. Please make sure outfits are tasteful and not too revealing. We don't want any stray gonads popping out of our shorts on the stairs again, Brian.

Thanks x

Hi all,

To impress Ofsted we are going to keep an archive of excellent work. Each time you give a merit to a pupil for a piece of work it must be marked, standardised, scanned and uploaded to the folder on the VLE where nobody will ever look at it again.

Thanks x

Hi all,

Please be aware that if the Principal greets you there are protocols to follow. There is a script in the Staff Handbook you should have learned (Who you're allowed to talk to, pages 45-249). All staff will take part in a role play exercise as a part of Appraisal.

Thanks x

Hi all,

Don't forget this week is Appraisal Observations, even though everyone has been observed at least twice since half term in the Mocksteds and Deep Dives. A member of SLT will come to your room a day later than agreed and slate your lesson in front of the pupils.

Thanks x

Hi all,

Just to let you know that the awful, overpowering smell around The Academy over the last few days has been from the canteen. They're getting ready for Christmas Dinner on the 21st of December and have put the sprouts on so they'll be ready in time.

Thanks x

Hi all,

This week's Well-Being Wednesday Activity is going to be fun. All staff must meet at 6:45am in the swimming pool for Waterobics, Tai Chi and a brisk 15 lengths before staff briefing at 7:45. This is a compulsory part of your Appraisal.

Thanks x

Hi all,

Just to let you know that Dominic's medication has changed again. He needs to take 5 Ritalin, 2 Celexa, 3 Paxil, and 1 Klonopin. If he starts kicking off, calmly guide him to the staffroom. Mrs Richards will cover his classes and his wife will come and collect him.

Thanks x

Hi all,

Due to budget cuts and utilities bills rising, we are cutting our CPD with immediate effect. All CPD will be planned and led by Willows Leaders and Google searches, so we'll never improve as an Academy or as individual teachers. SLT CPD will continue as normal.

Thanks x

Hi SLT,

Can we please check all emails before we send them to staff? This week there's been a number of emails with apostrophes in the right places, children's names spelled correctly, and 5 uses of the word "specifically" rather than "pacifically". This has to end now.

Thanks x

Hi all,

There have been a few queries about this week's calendar. It does say that there should be Core Subjects Deep Dive and a Core Subjects Mocksted. I can confirm we will be doing both. Mocksted Monday and Tuesday and Deep Dives from Wednesday. Feedback in January.

Thanks x

Hi all,
As a part of our ongoing Well-Being Programme we are going to introduce "Headteacher's Reward Tea". Colleagues who go "above and beyond" will be treated to cakes and sandwiches on Friday afternoons. You can nominate a colleague to receive HRT by using the VLE link.
Thanks x

Hi all,
Please congratulate Steve. He's just been appointed Assistant Assistant Vice Principal In Charge Of Assistant Assistant Assistant Vice Principals. There was a strong field but the monosyllabicity of his answers, the blueness of his suit and the brownness of his shoes won the panel over.
Thanks x

Hi all,
This week's Employee of the Week award goes to Mrs Simpkins. She has given out almost fifteen times as many merit points as anyone else this week, not a single behaviour point and has still never used the On Call. You could all take a leaf out of her book.
Thanks x

Hi all,
There was another error in this week's Academy newsletter. The local Army Cadet Corps is looking to recruit and train young people wanting to become buglers, not burglars. You'd need to see Chantelle's Uncle Brian for that.
Thanks x

Hi all,
We're making changes to the On Call System from Monday. It must only be used in extreme cases. You will fill in the On Call Google Form as usual and then you'll be put in a triage queue, where your case will be assessed by 5 members of SLT who won't come to help.
Thanks x

Hi all,
Sadly, one of our Teach First trainees has decided to leave The Academy. He didn't think he should just be covering the absences of 9Z's teachers. This means that until we can get some PGCE students we are going to have to use you all for cover during your frees.
Thanks x

Hi all,
Thanks for entering the current data into all the Data Spreadsheets folders on the VLE. We really are grateful. However, our Vice Principal in charge of data and tracking has asked that it also goes into the five new columns in sims. You have until 3:30pm today.
Thanks x

Hi all,
If you are a current Associate Associate Assistant Headteacher or have aspirations to be one, Miss Perkins will be putting on some Walking Around In Ridiculously Inappropriate High Heeled Shoes Thinking You're Special Training after school on Thursday.
Thanks x

Hi all,

I'm pleased to report that yesterday's 9Z RE trip to the local mosque was a total success. This is mainly down to the fact that we relieved Chantelle of her "Free shoes. Please help yourselves." sign before she got on the minibus.

Thanks x

Hi all,

On Thursday 9Z will all be doing their First Aid refresher course. Please keep an eye on the weedy kids until then, as last year, Boy Jayden thought it would be a good idea to create some real victims to practise on.

Thanks x

Hi all,

Since Covid we have allowed students to wear their PE kit on days when they have PE. Can you please remind your groups that this is not the case when they have swimming. It's getting a little cold for that now.

Thanks x

Hi all,

Because of tomorrow's Mocksted, Well-Being Wednesday has been cancelled this week. Tuesday's twilight CPD and Thursday's Year 7 Parents' Evening will go ahead as planned.

Thanks x

Hi all,

Please refer to page 1250, paragraphs 17-35 of the staff handbook when planning. Anyone who mentions the C word before the 20th of December will get a written warning. Also, when we find out who left Christmas wordsearches in Reprographics, they will be sacked.

Thanks x

Hi all,

Today's Learning Walks have shown not all pupils have the correct equipment in lessons. It is the responsibility of teachers to ensure that all children are given the right materials to succeed. While you're at it, why not do the work for them as well?

Thanks x

Hi all,

Just a reminder for teachers of 7Z: Brodie can't sit near Cody, Bodie or Jodie but can sit with Neve, Caimh and Steve. Sarah hates Zara and Sara but not Cara. Skyler, Tyler and Taylor should be OK together and Jeremy bites so needs to be alone or have his dog toy.

Thanks x

Hi all,

Can you please make sure that when you are not near your school computer, that you log out of The Academy network. We don't want any more incidents of 9Z using your departmental budgets to bulk buy strawberry marshmallow vapes, Monster energy drink or Lambrini.

Thanks x

Hi all,

Apparently, Ofsted don't like the new booths in the Removal Suite. They claim that they're restricting students' freedom to move and breach all kinds of human rights legislation. Luckily, the local pet shop has agreed to take them back and give us a full refund.

Thanks x

Hi all,

Today's Year 7 Spelling Bee didn't go quite to plan. The pupils were unaware that they'd be asked to spell other words, not just "bee"

Thanks x

Hi all,

Thanks to the MFL department for the European Languages Day multicultural activities this week. This week's two finger Kitkat is theirs. It's back to boring old French lessons with tedious verb and vocab lists now. Don't they know that everyone speaks English?

Thanks x

Hi all,

To motivate you to write your Year 7 "Settling In" Reports on time, we've created a competition. The teacher whose reports are the most indifferent and read like you have never met the kids in your life, will receive a hot drink of their choice from the canteen.

Thanks x

Hi all,
From next year we will only run a GCSE subject if there is a minimum of 35 pupils opting for it. So, if you are a minority subject, you have almost a full year to start to knobble the opposition. The most creative among you may just get to keep your jobs.
Thanks x

Hi all,
Tonight's CPD is Marking: Improving Learning Feedback. Mr Johnson will be sharing advice and anecdotes on how he has successfully become The Academy's MILF expert.
Thanks x

Hi all,
We have decided to follow the Government's advice and ban mobile phones for all pupils in all classrooms in The Academy from today. We're also banning drugs, smoking, vaping, knives and wasps.
Thanks x

Hi all,
Mr Johnson is having a meeting this afternoon for all of you interested in the Audit for Numeracy and Literacy currently underway. It's a part of our Learning, Understanding and Boosting Excellence programme. That's ANAL LUBE at 4pm.
Thanks x

Hi parents,
Our social media accounts have been hacked again. Please do not send in any more urine samples. We are not really drug testing pupils before the Inter House Sports Day. The empty jars have been donated to the Food Tech Department for when they do jam making.
Thanks x

Hi all,
We have now decided that we will run a GCSE Geography course this year. It was touch and go whether it would run but we found a huge box of coloured pencils in the big skip round the back of the kitchens, so we'd be crazy not to.
Thanks x

Hi parents,
Thank you for contributing to our Uniform Appeal, donating uniform items to help those families who are struggling at this time. We were, however, only expecting old Academy uniforms. Two of our Year 8s have been dressed as a vicar and a sexy nurse all week.
Thanks x

Hi all,
From Monday KS4 lunch detentions are to be used for giving pupils support to help them achieve. Our new initiative "Midday Detentions Maximise Achievement" is already causing excitement with Year 11. The "Sign up here for MDMA" posters seems to have attracted a lot of staff signatures, too.
Thanks x

Hi all,
We are five weeks in and our Book Looks show that there's not enough written work being done in some subjects. Also, we're still waiting for book samples from Music, Art and PE. They must be in the Board Room by 8:30am.
Thanks x

Hi all,
From Monday, we will no longer be using the "We All Now Know" acronym as our end of lessons plenary title as some parents have complained. We are going to go with "This Is Today's Summary" instead. So, we expect TITS to replace WANK in all lessons.
Thanks x

Hi all,
Those of you who buy stock for your departments will notice that, from Monday, we've added another 2 levels of pointless bureaucracy to the ordering process. This will save us money, as you'll inevitably give up and just go out and buy it all with your own money.
Thanks x

Hi all,
9Z refuse to believe that Mr Johnson has left The Academy and are convinced that he has been "done in" and his remains are somewhere on the premises. We can use this to our advantage to get them to tidy out all our cupboards and stockrooms. Sign up in the office.
Thanks x

Hi all,

Tomorrow's CPD has been cancelled so that you can prepare for Tuesday's Year 6 Open Evening. You will spend the three hours cleaning, polishing and redecorating your classrooms and Departmental areas. SLT will inspect them before you will be allowed to go home.

Thanks x

Hi all,

Sadly, the new stained glass window showing our CEO as the Messiah, and clutching The Academy Staff Handbook, has fallen out of its frame and smashed into a million pieces. It is not "an act of God" but a victim of 9Z putty theft. Art are doing mosaics this week.

Thanks x

Hi all,

Appraisal Round 3 starts this week. You'll each be observed during a randomly chosen lesson and three members of SLT will spend 5 minutes in your room. Each one of them will grade your lesson differently and we will choose the lowest. Feedback will not be given. Thanks x

Hi all,

Due to some kind of technical loophole, we have to reinstate Well-Being Wednesday. At Daily Briefing we will play a sound clip of some whale song and for those on duty at break time, if it is raining, we will lend you an Academy Umbrella. (Just on Wednesdays. Obvs.)

Thanks x

Hi all,

We're looking for a Behaviour Manager to play bad cop to Mr Johnson's good cop. The role involves a lot of shouting, harsh punishments, and following our 15 step behaviour policy to the letter. You'll leave after 3 months due to a total lack of support from SLT.

Thanks x

Hi all,

Please congratulate Mr Johnson on becoming our new Assistant Associate Assistant Associate Vice Principal's Assistant's Vice Principal. He will be off tomorrow to get fitted for a shiny blue suit and some scruffy brown shoes, one of which will have a black lace.

Thanks x

Hi all,

Yesterday was Mental Health Awareness Day. We asked you to watch three 1 hour mental health videos and complete the feedback sheets for each one. Some of you still haven't done this. Don't go home until you have done it.

Thanks x

Hi all,

Key Stage 3 exams are next week. For Year 9, make sure at you are giving the pupils a full GCSE paper, so we can gauge how much they know of a course they've never studied. This will help us to put in after school and half term intervention lessons for them.

Thanks x

Hi all,

Apparently, it would seem your Unions think we should be giving you feedback when we observe your lessons for Appraisal. So to save time, you'll get an email with one of these phrases:

- I liked it.
- I've seen better.
- Not very good.
- Meh.
- What do I know, I'm a PE teacher.

Thanks x

Hi all,

The new Head of Geography has complained that we are constantly belittling her department and has demanded an apology. Here is our apology: We are truly sorry she feels this.

Thanks x

PS If you're a geography teacher, "belittling" means "making fun of" or "ridiculing".

Hi all,

We have redefined the term "specialist" in the Staff Handbook. From next term, anyone with a GCSE in any subject, or if they did it at primary school, will be considered "a specialist" and will be expected to teach those subjects like an outstanding practitioner.

Thanks x

Hi all,

From Monday, one lucky teacher will get extra time each week to study new education incentives. This Weekly Hour Of Research into Education could help to further your career. If you are interested in The Academy WHORE scheme, speak to Janice, our resident expert.

Thanks x

Hi all,

The Academy's swimming pool will be back in action from Monday. The engineers have been out and, when unblocking the filter, discovered fifteen Academy blazers, 25 pairs of goggles, five bikini tops, 7 odd shoes, and 9Z's Maths exercise books from last term.

Thanks x

Hi all,

After half term, we are restructuring again. We are going to put everyone with a TLR on the management scale at L1. It'll look great on their CV, we won't have to give them PPA time, holidays or a lunch break and we'll save an absolute fortune.

Thanks x

Hi all,

Our new toilet policy starts tomorrow. Due to recent vandalism, no children are to go to the toilet during lessons. Except those with a medical pass. Or those with a note from their parents. And girls, they must be allowed to go. And boys. But no one else.

Thanks x

Printed in Great Britain
by Amazon

32510896R00099